图书在版编目（CIP）数据
永恒的美丽：美国平民诗选 / 沔牯佬编译 .
上海：同济大学出版社，2024.1
ISBN 978-7-5765-0602-0
Ⅰ . ①永… Ⅱ . ①沔… Ⅲ . ①诗集－美国 Ⅳ . ① I712.2
中国国家版本馆 CIP 数据核字（2023）第 159775 号

永恒的美丽

——美国平民诗选

沔 牯 佬　编译

出版策划：《民间影像》
责任编辑：陈立群（clq8384@126.com）
装帧设计：景嵘设计
电脑制作：朱丹天
责任校对：徐春莲

出版发行：同济大学出版社
地　　址：上海市杨浦区四平路 1239 号
电　　话：021-65985622
邮政编码：200092
网　　址：www.tongjipress.com.cn
经　　销：全国各地新华书店
印　　刷：上海锦良印刷厂
成品尺寸：143mm × 213mm　352 面
字　　数：296 000
版　　次：2024 年 1 月第 1 版
印　　次：2024 年 1 月第 1 次印刷
书　　号：ISBN 978-7-5765-0602-0
定　　价：78.00 元

Beauty That Is Never Old

永恒的美丽

——美国平民诗选

沔牯佬　编译

同济大学出版社·上海

序　一

难以
从诗中获得信息
然而男人每天都在可怜地死去
因为缺乏
诗的意境和美丽。

美国诗人威廉·卡罗斯·威廉姆斯这首常被引用的诗歌中有关“男人”的描述同样也适用于女性诗人、少数民族或土著部落，或者其他长期被禁言、边缘化和忽视的人们。李国华博士编译的这本《永恒的美丽——美国平民诗选》，收入百余首美国诗歌，其所传递的信息不仅关乎我们的个体生命，对人类社群健全的理智、情感和精神也不可或缺。在目前人类历史和地球生命所处的关键时刻，将这些美国诗歌介绍给中国读者对中美两国人民的相互了解尤为珍贵。

当面临动荡、危机、失落、焦虑与恐惧的时候，我们从诗歌中寻找明晰和慰藉。无论所处境遇是公众的还是个人遇到挑战，诗歌带有音乐性的激情澎湃语言总会帮助我们振奋精神，坚持下去。犹如沙漠中的绿洲，寒冬之夜熊熊燃烧的壁炉，困境中挣扎时的生命线，以及迷茫中的峰回路转，诗歌一次又一次拯救我们于危难之中。我们从中得到支持而变得强大。我们的呼声得到回应，得到温暖、安慰和食粮。

当然，并不是诗歌中所有的“信息”都令人生畏。另一名美国诗人罗伯特·弗罗斯特曾宣称，诗歌只是抵御迷茫困惑的短暂停留。难道这就是诗歌的唯一功能和使命吗？不是，绝对不是。从春天的第一朵纤细紫色的番红花到令人惊叹的崎岖山峰，诗歌引领我们去赞赏和思考大自然的壮丽辉煌。诗歌能够提醒我们感激铭记生命中充满希望和喜悦的时刻。正如其能够承载我们内心深处的恐惧和渴望，诗歌也能够表达我们的欣喜和赞美。

《永恒的美丽——美国平民诗选》这部题材多样的美国诗集出

自译者一个无比宽厚善良的动机——为那些因性别、种族和政治原因而被忽视或禁言，或者仅仅因文学鉴赏趣味的变化而被遗忘在历史长河中的诗人发声。无名之辈的作品与那些被收入诗歌年鉴和受人追棒的诗人之作在这部诗集中一同呈现。初次接触美国文学的读者可以通过这部诗集了解众多不同风格流派的美国诗歌。而已涉猎美国诗歌的读者将在这部诗集中发现自己偏爱的作品，他们所熟知诗人的新作及他们以前从未遇见过的陌生诗人的作品。

当然还存在第三种可能。艾米莉·狄金森生前默默无闻，几乎没有发表任何作品，现在被公认为是与沃尔特·惠特曼一起彻底改变了美国诗歌的诗人，让美国诗歌的主题和句法结构从英国传统中脱离出来。这部诗集中的无名诗人哪一位将会在未来某一天脱颖而出而成为下一个狄金森？是梅多拉·爱迪生？还是卢西安·沃特金斯？读者可以在这部值得关注的诗集中与他们相会。

这部诗集的出版非常及时而且亟需。我们生活在气候危机和国际关系紧张的不祥时代。将来会有足够的水用以满足人口、牲畜和农作物所需吗？我们是否为应对下一个瘟疫大流行或自然灾害做好准备？我们将会欢迎逃避这些灾难的移民吗？我们将怎样抚养我们的孩子、照顾我们的老人、保护我们的文化遗产？虽然这里可能没有回答这些生存性问题的具体方案，但我们现在比任何时候都需要诗歌。

更重要的是诗歌能帮助我们相互理解，共同应对人类所面临的前所未有的危胁。正如美国桂冠诗人特蕾西·K·史密斯在《美国日志，我们时代的五十首诗歌》的引言中写道：“我为什么热爱诗歌？它们要求我静坐、倾听，以及想象将自己放在某个陌生环境。鉴赏完一首诗歌之后，我重新回归的这个世界似乎因此变得更加丰富和可以理解。”

如果没有诗歌，我们会变得情感枯竭和精神颓废。诗歌滋长我们的韧性，培育我们的想象力。诗歌将我们从苦恼和孤独中解脱出来，缓解痛苦疲劳，振奋精神。最重要的是，诗歌激励我们去思考。《永恒的美丽——美国平民诗选》将让您感受诗歌对人性的所有承诺。

玛可辛·G·西尔维曼

2022 年 11 月 11 日于纽约

Preface

It is difficult
to get news from poems
yet men die miserably every day
for lack
of what is found there.

What the American poet William Carlos Williams observed about "men" in this frequently quoted poem is also true for poets who are women, people from minority or indigenous communities, or others traditionally silenced, marginalized, and neglected. *Beauty That Is Never Old*, over 100 poems translated into Mandarin by Dr. Guohua Li, conveys the news which is crucial not only to our personal lives, but also to the wellbeing—intellectual, emotional and spiritual—of our human community. Translating American poetry for Chinese readers seems especially important at this momentous time in human history and in the life of our planet.

Faced with upheaval, crisis, loss, anxiety, and dread, we reach for poetry for clarity and solace. Whether the circumstances are a public or personal challenge, poetry provides immediate and evocative language accompanied by verbal music to refresh and shore us up. An oasis in the desert, bright hearth on a bitter winter night, lifeline to those floundering, desire path in confusion—poetry rescues us again and again. We are braced and strengthened. We are heard. We have been warmed, comforted, and fed.

To be sure, not all the "news" is daunting. Another American poet, Robert Frost, declared that "a poem is a momentary stay against confusion." Is that poetry's only function, her only mission? No, surely not. From the first delicate purple crocus of spring to rugged, awe–inspiring mountain peaks, poetry issues an invitation to admire and reflect on nature's splendors. Poetry can serve to remind us to acknowledge and remember hopeful, joyous occasions. Just as she can hold our deepest fear and longing, poetry can also be the vessel of our rejoicing and our praise.

Beauty That Is Never Old, an eclectic gathering of American poems, is generated from a profoundly generous impulse to give voice to poets who were ignored, or silenced, in their own time for reasons of sex, race, and politics, or who were simply lost in time as literary taste changed. Lesser known or obscure poets are presented alongside those more often anthologized and celebrated. To the uninitiated, these poems will introduce American poetry in all its variety. Readers already familiar with American verse will find their favorites and discover new work by poets they know well and new poets they have not yet encountered.

There is a third possibility. Emily Dickinson, unknown and virtually unpublished in her lifetime, is recognized today as the poet who, along with Walt Whitman, revolutionized American poetry and distinguished American themes and syntax from roots in the British tradition. Who among the unknown poets in this volume will emerge one day as the next Dickinson? Medora Addison? Lucian Watkins? Meet them here in the translations of this note–worthy anthology.

How timely and welcome! We are living in an age of climate crisis and ominous global tensions. Will there be sufficient water for people, their livestock and crops? Are we ready for the next pandemic? The next natural disaster? Will we welcome immigrants fleeing these dangers? How will we provide for our children, care for our elders, and safeguard our cultural heritages? Although there may not be specific answers to such complex existential questions in these pages, we need poetry now more than ever.

And we need to understand each other, fellow human beings and citizens of a shared world that seems imperiled as never before. As Tracy K. Smith, former Poet Laureate of the United States, writes in her introduction to *American Journal*: *Fifty Poems for Our Time*, "This is why I love poems: they require me to sit still, listen deeply, and imagine putting myself in someone else's unfamiliar shoes. The world I return to when the poem is over seems fuller and more comprehensible as a result."

Without poetry we are emotionally depleted and spiritually bereft. Poetry fosters resilience and nourishes imagination. Releasing us from anguish and isolation, poetry offers respite and renews our spirit. Most of all, poetry encourages us to wonder. *Beauty That Is Never Old* fulfills poetry's promise.

Maxine G. Silverman

New York
November 11, 2022
www.maxinegsilverman.com

序　二

一方宁谧的风景

认识李国华教授二十年了。他来自中国，先是在美国约翰·霍普金斯大学攻读学位，后应聘哥伦比亚大学，成为公共卫生领域顶尖学者。李教授为人质朴，待人真诚。近两三年，在 COVID-19 疫情肆虐的封闭期间，多少人忧心慌乱，他却利用余暇安静地沉浸于西方诗歌中，而且一首一首地译成中文作品。一名公共卫生学者而具有如此高的人文修养，岂不令人激赏！

这本诗集选译了许多 19 世纪到 20 世纪的诗歌，诗人大多名气不大，由此不难看出李教授选诗的独到眼光。他似乎发现了：不分古今中外，无论名位高下，诗的真髓就寄托于诗人的心。正如中国古老的《毛诗序》所云："诗者，志之所之也。在心为志，发言为诗。"诗集的副标题"美国平民诗选"，说明这些诗歌是出自一颗颗平凡而诚挚、纯粹、自然的诗心。一首一首翻阅，我仿佛跌入一个个隔了时空的美丽灵魂之中。其中有年少的、年老的，快乐的、悲伤的，激情的、失恋的，或咏物，或咏景，或咏人，或咏事，处处是直觉的心象，句句是浑然的性情之作。

在众声喧哗的现代，诗这种非常个人、非常小众的文学类别，继续以其孤独而优雅的姿态存在着，默默纾解宽慰人类的紧张与苦痛。瘟疫还在蔓延，物质主义炽热张扬，这样的年代，正需要像李教授这样的有心人，坚定地为我们默守着一方宁谧的风景。

林素芬　博士
慈济大学东方语文学系教授
2022 年 11 月 15 日于花莲

序　三

打开一扇心扉

非常荣幸为李国华编译的《永恒的美丽——美国平民诗选》写几句话。翻阅这些美国诗歌，彷佛为我打开一扇扇窗，带我走进一个未知的诗歌和诗人世界。这里，很少见到那些引领20世纪美国诗歌风骚、几乎全为白人男性诗人的名字，例如惠特曼、庞德、弗罗斯特、斯蒂文森、普拉斯、阿什贝利和摩尔。与其相反，这部诗集收录了众多女诗人和少数族裔诗人的作品。其中有些人受到过良好教育，有些人没进过学堂；有些人出自中产家庭，有些人一直在贫困中挣扎。在这部诗集中可以听到来自不同阶层的人们叙说他们各自的生活经历，包括外界的和内心的。这些诗人也许无足轻重。但是当他们聚集在一起时，就像从旧衣拆下一块块棉布拼接成鲜艳的被毯，向人们更真实地展示特定时空的生活理念和梦想。他们的文学声音可能不同于斯特茨·特克尔在其名著《工作着》中所收集的平民口述历史，但是同样展现一幅形形色色的美国人齐心协力不断建设共同家园的集体画面。

在阅读英文原作时，我不停通过万维网查寻作者的信息，他们的生卒日期、地点以及其生平。其履历中也谈到他们曾试图为与其类似的诗人编辑年鉴。这些默默无闻的诗人在文学的聚光灯外写作，在临时性文学刊物上发表作品。如果能将他们为自己编辑的年鉴汇集起来，那么其作品就有更多机会被传承到不久的将来。他们的这种努力与国华所做的事情十分相似，虽然其目的是将这些作品介绍给一个不同文化背景下的读者，并将它们以数码形式保存下来。数码应该比发霉书堆中发黄的纸页更耐久。编译肯定与创作本身有许多相似之处。

这样的话，我必须在这里谈谈编译者的个人经历。国华来自湖北省的偏远地区。他凭借聪明勤奋从北京医科大学毕业，然后在位于美国巴尔迪摩的约翰·霍普金斯大学获公共卫生博士学位，其后到哥伦比亚大学任教。虽然这样高强度的学术工作似乎与文学毫不相关，但是医学与诗歌的联系其实普遍存在。济慈放弃行医去追求一个浪漫的梦想，而诸如威廉·卡罗斯·威廉姆斯、梅里尔·摩尔或安东·契诃夫等人将临床服务与写作集于一身，长年乐此不疲。国华虽然在此仅限于编译，他也从事诗歌创作并发表了一些作品。医生关注人类状况和社会形势的眼睛里可能有一根神经连接着作家和翻译家手中的笔。

贝克定　博士

东华大学历史系教授

2022 年 11 月 19 日于花莲

"Opening a Door"

It is an honor to say a few words of introduction to Guohua Li's collection of translations from American poetry. Leafing through the poems that Guohua collects here has opened a window for me into a previously unknown world of poetry and of poets. Here the familiar names of Whitman, Pound, Frost, Stevens, Plath, Ashbery, Moore, or other of the lily-white and almost-entirely-male authors to whom is ascribed the "canon" of Twentieth Century American poetry barely appear. No, this book is filled with the works of women and people of color, some well-educated and some not, some well-off economically and some who struggled. It is a broad spectrum of people speaking about what they see in their worlds, both around them and inside of them. Such poets might be said to be "minor", but when collected, pieced together like squares of cotton from old clothing to make a vibrant quilt, they give a far truer idea of the lives and aspirations of people in that place and through those times. The literary voices here may differ from the common speech collected by Studs Terkel in masterpieces such as *Working*, but the collective impression of a diverse American people coming together in the continuing task of forging a nation is much the same.

Reading through the English originals, I kept going back to the internet to see who was this or that author, where or when did they live, what was their life like. Their biographies also mention some of their efforts at preparing anthologies of poets who, like them, were writing outside of the literary spotlight, publishing in ephemeral literary journals, assembling these anthologies so that the works and their authors might have a better chance to pass on into the future "around the bend". This is much as Guohua does, though he here is also making the works accessible to a different cultural audience and preserving them in a digital form that will outlast the yellowed pages in musty bookstacks. Anthologizing, it seems, must be something like an act of authorship in itself.

And thus, this introduction would hardly be complete without a mention of the anthologist–translator's own journey. Coming from a rural area of Hubei province, Guohua's intelligence and dedication took him to a medical degree at the prestigious Beijing Medical University, then to Johns Hopkins University in Baltimore for a doctorate in public health, and finally to his current position as a professor in Columbia University. Though such intensive academic work might seem a world apart from literature, a connection between medicine and poetry is surprisingly common. Although Keats gave up his medical practice to follow a romantic vision, others – such as William Carlos Williams, Merrill Moore or Anton Chekov combined a continued dedication to their calling as physicians with a commitment to writing throughout their life. And it should be no surprise that, though he modestly refrains from translating them here, Guohua also has had poems published. The physician's eye for the human condition and the social situation may have a direct nerve connecting to the author–translator's pen.

Tim Baker, PhD
Professor
Department of History
Dong Hwa University
Hualien, Taiwan
November 19, 2022

目　录

未来的光阴

梅多拉·爱迪生①

我要用沉默之美充填我的灵魂，
　　高山与流云，
洒满阳光的山丘和阴暗的森林，
　　黎明，黄昏和夜空的点点繁星。

我要用宁静的音乐充满我的心，
　　山林中微风轻轻地吟唱，
黑夜里雨滴缓缓地奏鸣，
　　暮色寂静树林里画眉悠扬的歌声。

我要用美充满未来的光阴，
　　前途犹如东方天空一样光明；
在最黑暗的夜晚，我将看到满天繁星，
　　当音乐消亡时，我仍将听到画眉的歌声。

① 1891 ~ 1965，生于马萨诸塞州，1921 年度耶鲁大学青年诗人竞赛大奖获得者。文学作品包括诗集《梦想与利剑》。

The Days to Come

Medora C. Addison

Now shall I store my soul with silent beauty,
Beauty of drifting clouds and mountain heights,
Beauty of sun–splashed hills and shadowed forests,
Beauty of dawn and dusk and star–swept nights.

Now shall I fill my heart with quiet music,
Song of the wind across the pine–clad hill,
Song of the rain and, fairer than all music,
Call of the thrush when twilight woods are still.

So shall the days to come be filled with beauty,
Bright with the promise caught from eastern skies;
So shall I see the stars when night is darkest,
Still hear the thrush's song when music dies.

翅膀

利比·C. 贝尔[①]

像玫瑰一样，美梦好景不长，
　　迈着疾步无声离去；
犹如草叶上明亮的露珠，
　　在阳光下瞬间消亡。

就像百灵鸟的歌声一样，
　　穿越黎明的金色薄雾；
你闻之欲赏，
　　却已不知去向。

百灵鸟展开敏捷的翅膀，
　　追逐花开花放；
这就是为什么它边飞边唱，
　　来去匆忙。

我在梦中见到
　　一双蓝色的眼睛温柔明亮；
醒来之后知道
　　这是一个无法实现的梦想。

① 1849～1929，生于俄亥俄州。从小热爱文学，10岁起发表诗歌，1902年其诗集《梦幻之乡》出版。作品充满了对友情和人性的赞美。

百灵鸟不再在天空中飞翔，
　　它已随玫瑰与晨露消亡；
那张带着温柔目光的面容，
　　从未出现在我的视野而令我欣喜若狂。

在我的记忆中，
　　保留着所有美丽事物的印象；
我会不停地搜寻，
　　直到我的灵魂像百灵鸟一样找到它的翅膀。

When My Soul Findeth Wings

Libbie C. Baer

Like roses the bright dream did pass,
On swift, noiseless footsteps away;
Like glistening dew on the grass,
Dissolving beneath the sun's ray.

Like voice of the lark that doth soar,
Through the golden haze of the dawn;
You hear it and bend to adore,
Just hear it and then it is gone.

The lark on his swift, flashing wings,
Keeps pace with the flowers in their flight;
And that's why when soaring he sings,
And passes so swiftly from sight.

I slept, and a vision did see,
Of eyes that were tender and blue;
I awoke to know that for me
The vision may never come true.

The lark soars no more in the skies,
He's gone with the roses and dew;
The face with the soft tender eyes,
Comes never to gladden my view.

My memory holds images fair,
Of all these beautiful things;
Which I will be seeking somewhere,
When my soul, as lark, findeth wings.

圣诞之晨

利比·C. 贝尔

多么悲伤，多么高兴，
　　圣诞节的早晨！
也许有人说：“今天
　　亲爱的耶稣已经降生，
　　全世界充满了
　　希望与欢欣；
谁会感到悲伤
　　在这个圣诞节的早晨？”

多么高兴，多么伤心，
　　圣诞节的早晨！
也许有人说：“今天
　　亲爱的耶稣已经降生，
　　但是，哦，他死了，
　　死于十字架上的酷刑！
谁会感到高兴
　　在这个圣诞节的早晨？”

或者高兴，或者伤心，
　　在这个圣诞节的早晨，
对于一些人
　　圣诞意味欢乐与新生。
　　这短暂的生命
　　而对于其他人却意味死讯——
多么高兴，多么伤心，
　　在这个圣诞节的早晨。

Christmas Morn

Libbie C. Baer

How sad, how glad,
  The Christmas morn!
Some say, "To–day
  Dear Christ was born,
  And hope and mirth
  Flood all the earth;
Who would be sad
  This Christmas morn."

How glad, how sad,
  The Christmas morn!
"To–day," some say
  Dear Christ was born,
  But oh! He died;
  Was crucified!
Who could be glad
  This Christmas morn!

Or glad, or sad,
  This Christmas morn,
To some will come
  A joy new–born.
  The fleeting breath
  To some bring death,—
How glad, how sad
  This Christmas morn.

告别

路易丝·博根[①]

1.

没有什么被记住，也没有什么被忘记。
当我们醒来时，马车在温暖的夏日栈道上行驶，
窗台被夜雨淋湿，
鸟儿零栖在烟囱上
光怪陆离。

没有接受，也没有展望。
轻微的钟声按时敲响，
午后渐渐凉爽
人们聚集在荒芜的街道上。
天上挂着月亮，店前闪着灯光，
黄昏像雨雾一样下降。

双手紧握着双手
前额紧贴着前额——
别无所失，也别无所有
没有临别礼物 也没有委婉推就。

① 1897 ~ 1970，生于缅因州，从小热衷诗歌，19 岁在波士顿大学就读一年后辍学，迁居纽约追求文学创作。共出版六部诗集，1945 年被国会图书馆授予桂冠诗人称号，是首位获此殊荣的女性作家。

2.
我已将你铭记在心
你不是我偶尔访问过的小镇，
也不是我曾经走过的小径。

你如骨肉难舍难分
你比寒霜或烟灰还轻。

你是果皮
也是果汁，
你是歌曲和等待音乐的歌词。

3.
你已经知道了开始；
从我们每个人的经历。

聚集在一起；饱食，狂舞，忧郁，
酣睡，恐惧，坚持。
你知道这些生活方式。

到最后，就是厚颜无耻。
还有荒谬无稽——半途放弃；
气极败坏——但是无声无息
在寂静中独生闷气。
然后在黑夜里离去
没有火把，也没有油灯，
让你的别离留下几丝神秘。

Words for Departure

Louise Bogan

1.
Nothing was remembered, nothing forgotten.
When we awoke, wagons were passing on the warm summer pavements,
The window–sills were wet from rain in the night,
Birds scattered and settled over chimneypots
As among grotesque trees.

Nothing was accepted, nothing looked beyond.
Slight–voiced bells separated hour from hour,
The afternoon sifted coolness
And people drew together in streets becoming deserted.
There was a moon, and light in a shop–front,
And dusk falling like precipitous water.

Hand clasped hand,
Forehead still bowed to forehead—
Nothing was lost, nothing possessed,
There was no gift nor denial.

2.
I have remembered you.
You were not the town visited once,
Nor the road falling behind running feet.

You were as awkward as flesh
And lighter than frost or ashes.

You were the rind,
And the white–juiced apple,
The song, and the words waiting for music.

3.

You have learned the beginning;
Go from mine to the other.

Be together; eat, dance, despair,
Sleep, be threatened, endure.
You will know the way of that.

But at the end, be insolent;
Be absurd—strike the thing short off;
Be mad—only do not let talk
Wear the bloom from silence.
And go away without fire or lantern.
Let there be some uncertainty about your departure.

知 识

路易斯 · 博根

现在我才会意
激情如何难以温暖
禁锢中的肌体，
珍宝稍纵即逝——

我将躺在这里沉思
在它们伫立的大地，
树木如何投下一条长长的阴影
以及发出一声轻轻的叹息。

Knowledge

Louise Bogan

Now that I know
How passion warms little
Of flesh in the mould,
And treasure is brittle,—

I'll lie here and learn
How, over their ground,
Trees make a long shadow
And a light sound.

赐予

奥托·莱兰·勃哈南[1]

亲爱的，我不渴望独自拥有你，
　　将你迷人的魅力控制在我嫉妒的视线里；
去吧，将你的美丽祝福赐予世界
　　让其他的心也可以分享我的欢愉。

我不奢求，你的爱仅仅属于我自己
　　而其他人在沉闷的夜里哀声叹息；
去吧，亲吻流浪者的眼泪，
　　让其他的眼睛也可以感受光的欣喜。

在黑暗悲伤的日子里，
　　去吧，送去一个灿烂的微笑致意；
去吧，唱一首歌，友好地道一声问候，
　　让一些孤独痛苦的人得到温暖慰藉！

---

① 1895 ~ 1932，生于华盛顿特区，非裔诗人、歌手和作曲家，曾在纽约市一所高中任音乐教师。

Go Give the World

Otto Leland Bohanan

I do not crave to have thee mine alone, dear
Keeping thy charms within my jealous sight;
Go, give the world the blessing of thy beauty,
That other hearts may share of my delight!

I do not ask, thy love should be mine only
While others falter through the dreary night;
Go, kiss the tears from some wayfarer's vision,
That other eyes may know the joy of light!

Where days are sad and skies are hung with darkness,
Go, send a smile that sunshine may be rife;
Go, give a song, a word of kindly greeting,
To ease the sorrow of some lonely life!

维拉内拉

奥托·莱兰·勃哈南

寒风的尖叫哭嚎多么悲戚：
　　颤抖的阴影变得冰凉。
我的灵之魂啊，我曾经拥有你！

哦，闪亮的星星在哪里？
　　还有照亮山岭的月光？
寒风的尖叫哭嚎多么悲戚！

心中的绝望千丝万缕，
　　我的哭声怪异刺耳传向远方：
我的灵之魂啊，我曾经拥有你！

我已经饮尽激情狂酒的渣汁，
　　在我的屋檐房廊，
寒风的尖叫哭嚎多么悲戚！

你的梦想是神授天赐，
　　令人徒劳渴望；
我的灵之魂啊，我曾经拥有你！

我在这里恳求叹息
　　只为一个你永远不会实现的愿望；
寒风的尖叫哭嚎多么悲戚！
我的灵之魂啊，我曾经拥有你！

Villanelle

Otto Leland Bohanan

How dreary the winds shriek and whine:
The trembling shadows grow chill.
O soul of my soul, wert thou mine!

O where are the stars that did shine?
The moonlight that tinselled the hill?
How dreary the winds shriek and whine!

Despair'round my heart doth entwine,
Far soundeth my cry weird and shrill:
O soul of my soul, wert thou mine!

I've quaffed to the dregs the mad wine
Of passion, but under my sill
How dreary the winds shriek and whine!

'Tis thine, is the dream so divine,
That doth this vain yearning instill;
O soul of my soul, wert thou mine!

'Tis mine, here to crave and to pine
For what thou wilt never fulfill;
How dreary the winds shriek and whine!
O soul of my soul, wert thou mine!

长途

威廉·史丹利·布雷斯韦特[①]

海风吹过蓝色的水面，
　　前方的道路依然遥远。
但是我的心必须穿越更长的旅程，
　　在梦想成真之前。

我们必须热忱勤勉，
　　我们理应任劳任怨，
对于梦想的希望寄托，
　　使我们日复一日不断向前。

海风行走的路程很远，
　　但终会抵达陆地岸边。
时间的潮水流淌不停，
　　我的梦想永恒不变。

---

① 1878 ~ 1962，非裔作家、诗人、文学评论家和编辑，生于波士顿。其诗歌以抒情形式为主，其文学评论对 20 世纪初叶美国东海岸的诗歌创作风格具有非常重要的影响。

It Is a Long Way

William Stanley Braithwaite

It's a long way the sea–winds blow
 Over the sea–plains blue,—
But longer far has my heart to go
 Before its dreams come true.

It's work we must, and love we must,
 And do the best we may,
And take the hope of dreams in trust
 To keep us day by day.

It's a long way the sea–winds blow—
 But somewhere lies a shore—
Thus down the tide of Time shall flow
 My dreams forevermore.

我的生活

威廉·史丹利·布雷斯韦特

用美滋养我的灵魂往复不断；
让我的双手去干一件愉快的事情；
让我的心永远充满崭新的
白日梦想和奇幻；
爱所有具有知觉的生命，而且也
尊重那些无法避免的粗鲁和野蛮，
知道这个世界原本充满真与善——
而我的存在完全属于机遇偶然。

我的生活就是如此平凡：
一半像鲜花和芳草一样美满，
一半似恒星一样毫无变换。
相信在我告别人世的时候，
上帝会指引我迈进天堂的门坎，
我将不会留下任何遗憾和感叹！

This Is My Life

William Stanley Braithwaite

To feed my soul with beauty till I die;
To give my hands a pleasant task to do;
To keep my heart forever filled anew
With dreams and wonders which the days supply;
To love all conscious living, and thereby
Respect the brute who renders up its due,
And know the world as planned is good and true—
And thus —because there chanced to be an I!

This is my life since things are as they are:
One half akin to flowers and the grass:
The rest a law unto the changeless star.
And I believe when I shall come to pass
Within the Door His hand shall hold ajar
I'll leave no echoing whisper of Alas!

四月末

威廉·史丹利·布雷斯韦特

四月已近尾声
　　五月即将来临——
我的心啊，树林是如此阴森
　　在黄昏时分。

呓语声声
　　半梦半醒，
上帝窥视我的灵魂
　　看见一个闪亮升起的黎明。

四月已近尾声
　　转眼二十年光阴，
半梦半醒中的呓语
　　无踪无影。

Near the End of April

William Stanley Braithwaite

Near the End of April
    On the verge of May—
And o my heart, the woods were dusk
    At the close of day.

Half a word was spoken
    Out of half a dream,
And God looked in my soul and saw
    A dawn rise and gleam.

Near the end of April
    Twenty Mays have met,
And half a word and half a dream
    Remember and forget.

杉奈柯克的早晨

奥利维亚·沃德·布什－班克斯[1]

东升的太阳给山岭戴上皇冠，
　　为平原陡添美感；
哦，多么壮丽的奇观！
　　多么神秘的大自然！

我站在一片茂密的树林中凝望，
　　周围的景色不禁令我欣喜惊叹；
天空犹如一片无边的湛蓝，
　　从大海弥漫到远岸。

一望无际的玉米地，
　　如波浪一样起伏伸展。
小鸟在我的耳边轻声鸣唱，
　　欢迎又一个崭新的晨旦。

简朴的小屋，
　　在静谧中悠闲零散。
林中的枝叶，
　　在微风中舞姿款款。

哦，晨旦时光是如此甜蜜美满，
　　我多么希望你延续不断；
但是你渐渐被白天取代
　　令我记起往日的悲惨。

啊，多么公平的生活开端！
　　黎明时辰是如此欢乐温暖。
可是，一旦与悲痛的白日融合，
　　美丽便随着晨曦消散。

---

① 1869 ~ 1944，生于纽约长岛，父亲是黑人，母亲是印第安人蒙托克部落后裔。虽然年幼丧母，但她继承了父母的多元文化传统，成长为一名作家、诗人和新闻记者。

Morning on Shinnecock

Olivia Ward Bush–Banks

The rising sun had crowned the hills,
And added beauty to the plain;
O grand and wondrous spectacle!
That only nature could explain.

I stood within a leafy grove,
And gazed around in blissful awe;
The sky appeared one mass of blue,
That seemed to spread from sea to shore.

Far as the human eye could see,
Were stretched the fields of waving corn.
Soft on my ear the warbling birds
Were heralding the birth of morn.

While here and there a cottage quaint
Seemed to repose in quiet ease
Amid the trees, whose leaflets waved
And fluttered in the passing breeze.

O morning hour! so dear thy joy,
And how I longed for thee to last;
But e'en thy fading into day
Brought me an echo of the past.

'Twas this,—how fair my life began;
How pleasant was its hour of dawn;
But, merging into sorrow's day,
Then beauty faded with the morn.

遗憾

奥利维亚·沃德·布什－班克斯

那天我说了一句轻率的话语，
亲爱的人闻之便离我而去；
我恳求道：“请原谅我，我并非恶意；
我不是故意伤害你。”
我徒劳地等待了很久，
盼望我的爱人回心转意。
但是为时已晚，无论祈祷还是哭泣；
死神来临，我的爱人溘然长逝。
我的命运是怎样的痛苦；
我的悲伤无法用语言定义；
悔恨的泪水无法收回
那天我未加思考所说的几个字。

Regret

Olivia Ward Bush-Banks

I said a thoughtless word one day,
A loved one heard and went away;
I cried: “Forgive me, I was blind;
I would not wound or be unkind.”
I waited long, but all in vain,
To win my loved one back again.
Too late, alas! to weep and pray,
Death came; my loved one passed away.
Then, what a bitter fate was mine;
No language could my grief define;
Tears of deep regret could not unsay
The thoughtless word I spoke that day.

闪电

威特·拜纳[1]

与你见面我有一种孤独感，
当你离开之后感觉仍然有你相伴。
你犹如天堂里戴着面纱的闪电，
我看见你的美丽惊艳
为时已晚。
与你见面我有一种失明感，
当你离开之后看到你的倩影依然。

Lightning

Witter Bynner

There is a solitude in seeing you,
Followed by your company when you are gone.
You are like heaven's veils of lightning.
I cannot see till afterward
How beautiful you are.
There is a blindness in seeing you,
Followed by the sight of you when you are gone.

---

① 1881 ~ 1968，独立诗人和翻译家。生于纽约布鲁克林，哈佛大学毕业，曾任教加利福尼亚大学伯克利分校，长期与中国学者江亢虎合作将唐诗译成英文在西方出版。

抚 摸

威特·拜纳

抚摸的时候，
你犹如一个敏捷的弓箭手，
欣悦之箭将我的整个身体穿透。

你是山泉，
我是崖缘，
一道闪亮的瀑布跃过我的眼前。

At the Touch of You

Witter Bynner

At the touch of you,
As if you were an archer with your swift hand at the bow,
The arrows of delight shot through my body.

You were spring,
And I the edge of a cliff,
And a shining waterfall rushed over me.

幻想

米诺特·卡特夫人[①]

如果我们能从最后的长眠中归来
去寻找我们曾经的至爱，
当然不是以令他们害怕的方式，
而是轻轻地让他们感到我们的亲密。

我们是否会化作傍晚的花香
带回心中往日的幸福时光？
我们是否会伴随哀鸽的悲歌归来
向他们重叙我们无尽的爱？

我们是否会化作清脆的雨滴
高兴地告诉他们我们将会重聚？
我们是否会在静静的落雪中归来
带着多年前的青春风彩？

我们是否会化作彩虹或晚霞
反复告诫他们求真辨假？
我们是否会伴随凄美的歌曲归来
让他们在快乐而不是痛苦中等待？

这些仅仅是微弱模糊的幻想；
因为我们怎敢质疑上帝的智慧荣光——
他以生命的代价给予我们甜蜜的胜利
让我们与所爱的人相聚在极乐世界里？

---

① 1878～？，是达科他部落印第安人，园艺爱好者和12个孩子的母亲。44岁时居住在加利福尼亚州，一位朋友将她的两首诗：*Fancies*（幻想）和*Raindrops*（雨滴）寄给当地印第安人首领而被发表。

Fancies

Mrs. Minot Carter

If we could return from our last long rest
And seek out the ones we loved the best,
Though not in a form to cause them fear,
Just gently to let them feel us near,

Would we come in the scent of the evening flowers
Bringing to mind past happy hours?
Would we come in the song of the mourning dove
Recalling to them our endless love?

Would we come in the sound of the falling rain
Telling them gladly "We shall meet again" ?
Would we come in the silently falling snow
With memories of rosy cheeks long ago?

Would we come in the rainbow or sunset's hue
Repeating to them "Be true, be true" ?
Would we speak in some sad sweet song's refrain
Bidding them wait in gladness, not pain?

These are but fancies, faint and dim;
For dare we question the wisdom of Him
Who gave us through death the victory sweet
To be with our loved ones in joy complete?

雨滴

米诺特·卡特夫人

你是否听到过雨点
　　掉落在玉米地里，
拍打着绿色的叶片
　　灰暗孤寂？
你曾否幻想
　　它们是一只只小脚
带着水匆匆忙忙
　　去拯救干渴的禾苗？

你是否见到过雨滴
　　掉落在湖面？
它们闪烁熠熠
　　让微小的水花飞溅。
你曾否幻想
　　它们是珍稀的钻石
被飞机播撒四方
　　在空中航行奔驰？

Raindrops

Mrs. Minot Carter

Have you heard the raindrops
    On a field of corn,
Pattering ov'r the green leaves
    Dusty and forlorn?
Did you ever fancy
    They were little feet
Hurrying out with water
    Thirsty ones to meet?

Have you seen the raindrops
    Falling on the lake?
How they flash and sparkle
    Tiny splashes make.
Did you ever fancy
    They were diamonds rare
Scattered by an aeroplane
    Sailing through the air?

音乐

艾丽丝·卡里[1]

你会听到音乐，肃穆深沉
　　飘过天穹
乌云，犹如义愤的千军万马
　　浩荡出征：
越过惊涛峻岭
　　众志成城，
无形之手在疯狂演奏
　　迸发激情。

充满真理和情感的回声
　　从远古游吟诗人的优美旋律中传来，
犹如神灵，在光天化日之下行窃于
　　破碎的历史残垣。
真理的回声穿越时空，
宇宙，辉煌宫殿般的宇宙
　　震颤亢奋，
就像盛开的花瓣上
　　蜜蜂嗡嗡哼唱的歌声。

空中，草原上的小鸟
　　——那些甜蜜歌声的化身——
留下它们明亮梦幻的倩影
　　和悠长金色的迹痕。
直到我们放下铠甲，
　　如同囚犯一般离开滚滚红尘，
灵魂里，音乐伴随着
　　心律奏鸣。

---

① 1820～1871，生长于俄亥俄州一个农场，17岁开始在报刊发表诗作，30岁时与同为诗人的妹妹菲碧·卡里一起迁居纽约，专事文学创作，代表作包括诗集《悲伤的孩子》。

Music

Alice Cary

There is music, deep and solemn
Floating through the vaulted arch
When, in many an angry column,
Clouds take up their stormy march:
O'er the ocean billows, heaping
Mountains on the sloping sands,
There are ever wildly sweeping
Shapeless and invisible hands.

Echoes full of truth and feeling
From the olden bards sublime,
Are, like spirits, brightly stealing
Through the broken walls of time.
The universe, that glorious palace,
Thrills and trembles as they float,
Like the little blossom's chalice
With the humming of the mote.

On the air, as birds in meadows—
Sweet embodiments of song—
Leave their bright fantastic shadows
Trailing goldenly along.
Till, aside our armor laying,
We like prisoners depart,
In the soul is music playing
To the beating of the heart.

至爱唱晚

威拉·凯瑟[①]

亲爱的，世上万物之中
唯一值得你我念想的是什么，
　　除了爱，
　　除了爱？

白天是这么短暂，昼夜流逝飞快，
多么广阔的世界，如此深邃的大海，
　　如此黑暗的大海。

太阳和星星是那么遥远，
在它们的光芒之外啊，亲爱的，谁知道有多远，
　　谁知道有多远？

世事沧桑渺茫，唯一真实的，
我的心知道，将它告诉你，
　　将它告诉你。

生命是如此盲目，最后的安眠是那么漫长，
令我们欢笑或悲泣的只有爱，
　　除了爱，
　　只有爱。

---

① 1873～1947，生于弗吉尼亚州，6岁随父母迁居内布拉斯加州。作品以中西部大平原开荒者为主题的小说见长。她当过多年中学英文教师，33岁迁居纽约从事写作，并担任多家杂志编辑。

Evening Song

Willa Cather

Dear love, what thing of all the things that be
Is ever worth one thought from you or me,
    Save only Love,
    Save only Love?

The days so short, the nights so quick to flee,
The world so wide, so deep and dark the sea,
    So dark the sea;

So far the suns and every listless star,
Beyond their light—Ah! dear, who knows how far,
    Who knows how far?

One thing of all dim things I know is true,
The heart within me knows, and tells it you,
    And tells it you.

So blind is life, so long at last is sleep,
And none but Love to bid us laugh or weep,
    And none but Love,
    And none but Love.

携手

卡丽·威廉姆斯·克里弗德[1]

哦，来吧，爱神，让我们一起，
携手走向生命之旅；
途中可能会有风暴，
但是我们何必在乎什么天气。

碧空万里，
和煦的微风清香沁脾，
我们的欢笑声，
将回荡在山谷里。

生命的风暴来袭，
对我们无情打击，
我们会努力抗争，
用笑声表达对命运的蔑视。

我们将漫步生命之旅，
你我携手与爱相依，
我们会快乐幸福，
无论阳光明媚或疾风骤雨。

---

① 1862 ~ 1934，非裔女诗人和民权运动与女权主义倡导者，美国有色人种协进会早期领导人之一，成长于俄亥俄州。其诗作集中于对种族问题的思考和对人道与爱情的讴歌。

Together

Carrie Williams Clifford

O, come, Love, let us take a walk,
Down the Way–of–Life together;
Storms may come, but what care we,
If be fair or foul the weather.

When the sky overhead is blue,
Balmy, scented winds will after
Us, adown the valley blow
Haunting echoes of our laughter.

When Life's storms upon us beat
Crushing us with fury, after
All is done, there'll ringing come
Mocking echoes of our laughter.

So we'll walk the Way–of–Life,
You and I, Love, both together,
Storm or sunshine, happy we
If be foul or fair the weather.

探 索

卡丽 · 威廉姆斯 · 克里弗德

我的目标超越了最遥远的恒星，
但是它就深藏在我最隐秘的灵魂；
我是我的目标——我的探索是为了寻求自知之明。
在这茫茫大海中航行，
我必须洞察万象，探索不停。
我的灵魂包藏所有的思想，所有的奥秘
和所有伟大哲人的智慧神明：
为了发现，我必须扬帆起程，
最后在我搏动的心脏里找到本真。

Quest

Carrie Williams Clifford

My goal out-distances the utmost star,
Yet is encompassed in my inmost Soul;
I am my goal—my quest, to know myself.
To chart and compass this unfathomed sea,
Myself must plumb the boundless universe.
My Soul contains all thought, all mystery,
All wisdom of the Great Infinite Mind:
This is to discover, I must voyage far,
At last to find it in my pulsing heart.

生与死

卡丽·威廉姆斯·克里弗德

生

我看见房间烛光闪亮！
垂帘雅致大方，
窗子透明如水晶一样！
宽大的壁炉旁
笑谈中的机智诙谐
闪烁跳跃
轻快流淌，
音乐使温馨的气氛更加欢畅。
多么亲切的场景，
充满了生机，爱和光！

死

然后我看见乌云突现
愁绪占据了房间：
蓝灰色的薄雾笼罩了玻璃窗
挫败沮丧沉潜！
幽灵从阴影中走来，
烛光化作一缕青烟。

Life and Death

Carrie Williams Clifford

Life

I saw the candle brightly burning in the room!
The fringed curtains gracefully draped back,
The windows, crystal clear!
Upon the generous hearth
Quick Wit and bubbling Laughter
Flashed and danced
Sparkled and pranced,
And music to the glowing scene lent cheer.
It was a gracious sight,
So full of life, of love, of light.

Death

Then suddenly I saw a cloud of gloom
Take form within the room:
A blue–grey mist obscured the window–panes
And silent fell the rout!
Then from the shadows came the Dreaded Shape, —
The candle flickered out!

再见

佛罗伦丝·厄尔·科茨[1]

悲伤，请放弃我一会儿！
　　寒冬已经过去；
伴随着四月的微笑，紫罗兰和三叶草，
　　希望重新开始。

欢乐追随她的足迹，
　　爱飞奔而去，
小溪的音乐如此甜美，
　　犹如童年的欢声笑语。

枝头的小鸟
　　无法抑制它的欣喜，
含苞待放的花蕾
　　被美神尽收眼底。

悲伤，你是冬天的伴侣，
　　春天不会挽留你；
然而，啊，我的故友，
　　我不会将你忘记！

---

① 1850～1927，生于宾夕法尼亚州费城，年轻时曾留学法国巴黎，并在比利时布鲁塞尔学习音乐。她曾在各种报刊上发表了近300首诗，其中一部分被谱曲成为音乐作品。其诗歌赞美友情和大自然，并以借用希腊奥林匹亚人物讴歌第一次世界大战期间的英雄主义而著称。

An Adieu

Florence Earle Coates

Sorrow, quit me for a while!
    Wintry days are over;
Hope again, with April smile,
    Violets sows and clover.

Pleasure follows in her path,
    Love itself flies after,
And the brook a music hath
    Sweet as childhood's laughter.

Not a bird upon the bough
    Can repress its rapture,
Not a bud that blossoms now
    But doth beauty capture.

Sorrow, thou art Winter's mate,
    Spring cannot regret thee;
Yet, ah, yet—my friend of late—
    I shall not forget thee!

冬雨过后

艾娜·唐娜·库尔布里斯[①]

冬雨过后，
　　唱吧，歌鸲！唱吧，燕子！
绿草已经冒头，
　　花蕾即将开启。

林中将响起轻快的旋律，
　　伴随小鸟啼啭唧啾，
虽然今日天空仍在哭泣，
　　朔风凛冽依旧。

雷霆巨响
　　阵阵轰鸣，
狂风暴雨之上
　　白雾升腾；

波浪将会轻轻地到达
　　绵长明亮的海滨，
带着可爱的浪花
　　和温柔的涛声……

经过了冬天的痛苦惆怅
　　和漫长悲哀，
唱吧，心脏！——重新为你歌唱
　　欢乐伴随明天到来。

---

① 1841～1928，生于依利诺州一个摩门教家庭，年幼丧父，随母迁居加利福尼亚州，在洛杉矶长大，后定居旧金山湾区。11岁便开始发表诗歌，成为加利福尼亚州第一位桂冠诗人，被誉为加州甜蜜歌手，与小说家布勒特·哈特和诗人查尔斯·沃伦·斯托达特一起被称为金门三杰。

After the Winter Rain

Ina Donna Coolbrith

After the winter rain,
Sing, robin! Sing, swallow!
Grasses are in the lane,
Buds and flowers will follow.

Woods shall ring, blithe and gay,
With bird–trill and twitter,
Though the skies weep to–day,
And the winds are bitter.

Though deep call unto deep
As calls the thunder,
And white the billows leap
The tempest under;

Softly the waves shall come
Up the long, bright beaches,
With dainty, flowers of foam
And tenderest speeches...

After the wintry pain,
And the long, long sorrow,
Sing, heart!—for thee again
Joy comes with the morrow.

梦与歌

詹姆斯·D. 克罗瑟斯[①]

犹如动人的琵琶弹奏完繁花似锦的乐章，
我们的心弦常常恬静安详；
试图用乏味的辞藻来表达不可言喻的美，
我们久久冥思默想。
我们的激情多么虚无渺茫！
梦想美于歌唱。

被人讴歌赞颂的玫瑰
依然凋谢消亡。但是，从记忆的瓮缸，
缠绵的花朵温柔地
抱怨我们无稽的吟唱。
唉，我们尽管努力但是美丽反常！
梦比歌更加可爱令人神往。

难道雪莱未曾渴望金色的火焰？
难道济慈没有追逐美的幻想？
可悲的是我！
竟为花仙哀伤。
我相思已久——
梦想美于歌唱。

① 1869～1919，记者、诗人和牧师，生于密歇根州一小镇，曾就读西北大学，19世纪末和20世纪初美国著名黑人作家之一。

啊，我们虽然搭建了一个黎明的凉亭，
但是金翅鸟已经不知去向，
晨曦也许会透过枝叶
将乳燕啁啾的屋檐照亮。
什么艺术或黄金能够储藏延长
一个远比歌曲更美好的梦想？

梦想躁动的翅膀，
如同巫术上演在我们的胸膛；
但是亲爱的成就之神的目光
却注视着其他方向。那个追求已久的大奖，
我的琵琶，一定属于神灵独享。
梦想美于歌唱。

Dream and the Song

James D. Corrothers

So oft our hearts, belovè d lute,
In blossomy haunts of song are mute;
So long we pore, ’ mid murmurings dull,
O’er loveliness unutterable.
So vain is all our passion strong!
The dream is lovelier than the song.

The rose thought, touched by words, doth turn Wan ashes.
Still, from memory’s urn, The lingering blossoms tenderly
Refute our wilding minstrelsy.
Alas! We work but beauty’s wrong!
The dream is lovelier than the song.

Yearned Shelley o'er the golden flame?
Left Keats for beauty's lure, a name
But "writ in water" ? Woe is me!
To grieve o'er flowerful faëry.
My Phasian doves are flown so long—
The dream is lovelier than the song!

Ah, though we build a bower of dawn,
The golden-wingèd bird is gone,
And morn may gild, through shimmering leaves,
Only the swallow-twittering eaves.
What art may house or gold prolong
A dream far lovelier than a song?

The lilting witchery, the unrest
Of wingèd dreams, is in our breast;
But ever dear Fulfilment's eyes
Gaze otherward. The long-sought prize,
My lute, must to the gods belong.
The dream is lovelier than the song.

四月的一天

约瑟夫·塞蒙·小卡特尔[1]

如此美好的日子，如此美好的日子，
天地万物洋溢四月的极乐至喜，
和煦的微风轻柔地亲吻你的脸，
只要活着便足矣……在如此美好的一日！

An April Day

Joseph Seamon Cotter Jr.

On such a day as this I think, on such a day as this,
When earth and sky and nature's whole are clad in April's bliss;
And balmy zephyrs gently waft, upon your cheek, a kiss;
Sufficient is it just to live...on such a day as this!

① 1895 ~ 1919，年轻有为的黑人记者、剧作家和诗人，生于肯塔基州路易斯维尔市，大学期间不幸染上肺结核，英年早逝。

夙愿

约瑟夫·塞蒙·小卡特尔

我静卧在床，
仰面朝上；
无尽的浮想
在天花板上流淌——
童年的快乐无忧，
少年的沉思迷惘，
夫妻的夏夜明月，
母亲的圣洁容光，
老人的默默凝望
越过暮色苍茫。
上帝啊，请圆我做父亲的梦想。

A Prayer

Joseph Seamon Cotter Jr.

As I lie in bed,
Flat on my back;
There passes across my ceiling
An endless panorama of things—
Quick steps of gay-voiced children,
Adolescence in its wondering silences,
Maid and man on moonlit summer's eve,
Women in the holy glow of Motherhood,
Old men gazing silently thru the twilight
Into the beyond.
O God, give me words to make my dream-children live.

我的歌

约瑟夫·塞曼·大卡特尔[1]

我给自己唱一首歌，一首微妙的歌，
　　一首温暖我心灵的歌，
并将它放飞山川海河
　　去寻找一个欢乐之所。

我对我的歌说：“向前，向前，
　　找到一个灵魂的庇护所
那里没有仇恨
　　和自私的怒火。”

我的歌只走了短短的行程
　　便急忙回到了我身边；
它愧疚地倒在我的脚下
　　深受伤害折磨。

我凝视了一会便明白
　　到底发生了什么，
一个恶毒的评论家逮住了我的歌
　　将它抨击得丧魂失魄。

哦，人心确实可怜可恶
　　（它何必如此刻薄？）
在言辞外表下泰然自若，
　　在真理面前却张皇失措。

① 1861～1945，美国最早的黑人剧作家之一，肯塔基州第一位非裔诗人。生于肯塔基州，父亲是苏格兰人，母亲是黑人和印地安人后裔。他在贫困中长大，小学三年级后便辍学回家，从事各种繁重的体力劳动，22 岁时通过一年夜校学习获教师资格。之后一直从事黑人儿童教育工作。

My Song

Joseph Seamon Cotter Sr.

I sang me a song, a tiny song,
A song that was sweet to my soul,
And set it a–float on the sea of chance
In search of a happy goal.

I said to my song: "Go on, go on
And lodge in a tender spot
Of some human soul where the fires of hate
And selfishness are not."

My song went on but a little space
And hied it back to me;
And fell at my feet in a sorry plight—
The victim of cruelty.

I gazed a moment and quickly saw
Just how it had come about,
A cruel critic had caught my song
And probed the soul of it out.

O, poor indeed is the human mind
(And why was it ever wrought?)
That can thrive on husk in the form of words,
And not on a sturdy thought.

秋 夜

阿德莱德·克拉普西[①]

请听……
脆弱之声，
如幽灵的脚步，
霜叶纷纷离开枝头
飘零。

November Night

Adelaide Crapsey

Listen...
With faint dry sound,
Like steps of passing ghosts,
The leaves, frost–crisp'd, break from the trees
And fall.

① 1878 ~ 1914，生于纽约市布鲁克林区一个传教士家庭，幼年随父母迁居纽约上州罗切斯特市，瓦萨尔学院毕业并留学意大利罗马。受日本俳句启发和影响，作者创立了英文五行诗，各行分别由二、四、六、八、二个音节或单词组成。

伊尔哈布尔格言

阿德莱德·克拉普西

肉体
犹如蒸汽
随风而散又如
风前尘埃但我仍是
自己。

Saying of Il Haboul

Adelaide Crapsey

My tent
A vapour that
The wind dispels and but
As dust before the wind am I
Myself.

如果你离开

康梯·卡伦[①]

爱，轻轻地离我而去，
像静静流逝的时光；
我们毫无察觉，直到晚上，
才知道一天已成为以往。

曾经众多的希望，
已经名存实亡。
爱已不在，
亲爱的，你也远走他乡。

静静地离开，犹如一个梦想；
不留下任何痕迹，
除了一线微光
掠过做梦人的脸庞。

---

① 1903 ~ 1946，孤儿，出生地不详。9 岁时被亲戚带到纽约，15 岁被黑人牧师弗雷德里克·卡伦领养，先后就读纽约大学和哈佛大学，诗人、小说家、剧作家和儿童作家以及哈莱姆黑人文艺复兴运动重要成员。

If You Should Go

Countee Cullen

Love, leave me like the light,
The gently passing day;
We would not know, but for the night,
When it has slipped away.

So many hopes have fled,
Have left me but the name
Of what they were. When love is dead,
Go thou, beloved, the same.

Go quietly; a dream
When done, should leave no trace
That it has lived, except a gleam
Across the dreamer's face.

为一个诗人而作

康梯·卡伦

我将梦想用一块绸布包裹，
装进一个金盒隐藏埋没；
我将梦想用一块绸布包裹，
那里将长年遭受飞蛾咬嚼；
我没有掩盖仇恨；我本来就无怒火
我发现大地的呼吸是如此执着冷默；
我将梦想用一块绸布包裹，
装进一个金盒隐藏埋没。

For a Poet

Countee Cullen

I have wrapped my dreams in a silken cloth,
And laid them away in a box of gold;
Where long will cling the lips of the moth,
I have wrapped my dreams in a silken cloth;
I hide no hate; I am not even wroth
Who found earth's breath so keen and cold;
I have wrapped my dreams in a silken cloth,
And laid them away in a box of gold.

玫瑰花蕾之歌

康梯·卡伦

因为人到最后都会变得胆怯畏惧，
不再留意
春来秋去，
或垂落的冷雨，

所以花虽无意但我仍采摘几枝，
没有举杯但我仍啜吸，
因为嘴存最甘甜的糖果美食，
唇藏最陈旧的酒酿醪汁。

如果几年之后我已老去，
听到那首抱怨的歌曲
“呜呼哀哉”和“这般如此，
当我年轻时”，

我必须存留甜蜜的记忆，
困苦之中的花香鸟语，
以及一丝永不熄灭的薪火
点亮我的生命之旅。

Youth Sings a Song of Rosebud

Countee Cullen

Since men grow diffident at last,
And care no whit at all,If spring be come,
or the fall be past,Or how the cool rains fall,

I come to no flower but I pluck,
I raise no cup but I sip,
For a mouth is the best of sweets to suck;
The oldest wine's on the lip.

If I grow old in a year or two,
And come to the querulous song
Of 'Alack and aday' and 'This was true,
And that, when I was young,'

I must have sweets to remember by,
Some blossom saved from the mire,
Some death–rebellious ember I
Can fan into a fire.

感性

E.E. 卡明斯[①]

因为感觉第一
冷静理性
缜密思考的人
永远不会尽情亲吻你；

做一个十足的傻子
在春天的世界里

我的血液默许，
亲吻比理智
是更好的天意

女士，我用所有的鲜花发誓。
不用哭泣
—— 我能想到的最美姿势
不及你眼睑颤动所传的柔情蜜意
如果我们注定在一起
那么笑着依偎在我的怀抱里
因为生活不是三言两语

而且我相信死亡不是括号注释

---

① 1894 ~ 1962，诗人、画家和剧作家。出生马萨诸塞州剑桥镇，哈佛大学毕业。8 岁开始写诗，笔耕不辍，一生创作约 2900 首诗歌，是美国现代派自由体诗歌代表人物之一。他的诗歌一般不用大写字母，灵活运用语法和句法结构，题材丰富多彩。

since feeling is first

E. E. Cummings

since feeling is first
who pays any attention
to the syntax of things
will never wholly kiss you;

wholly to be a fool
while Spring is in the world

my blood approves,
and kisses are a better fate
than wisdom

lady i swear by all flowers. Don't cry
—the best gesture of my brain is less than
your eyelids' flutter which says
we are for each other: then
laugh, leaning back in my arms
for life's not a paragraph

And death i think is no parenthesis

暮光

卢克蕾迪亚·玛丽娅·戴卫森[①]

暮色时分是多么令人神往，
　　阳光带着沉思的阴影映照在傍晚的河面上；
内心的愉悦甜蜜酣畅，
　　犹如圣徒启程回到他们安息的地方。

噢，可爱的撒拉纳克河，
　　我愿在你的岸边徘徊遐想，
观赏最后一缕日光跳跃在你的波浪上，
　　目送白色的帆船轻快地掠过河湾或勇士的坟岗。

哦，静谧甜美的心轻盈开朗。
　　希望的前景光明，幻想美妙辉煌。
让我暂时停留在神奇的白日梦里，
　　记住缓缓西沉的最后缕缕阳光。

① 1808～1825，生于纽约州普拉茨堡镇。聪颖过人，少年老成，4岁起便沉溺阅读，7岁开始写作。不幸被肺结核夺去生命，年仅16岁。她短暂一生留下了近300首诗歌。《暮光》系其15岁时所作。

Twilight

Lucretia Maria Davidson

(Written in her fifteenth year)

How sweet the hour when daylight blends
With the pensive shadows on evening's breast;
And dear to the heart is the pleasure it lends,
For 'tis like the departure of saints to their rest.

Oh, 'tis sweet, Saranac, on thy loved banks to stray
To watch the last day–beam dance light on thy wave,
To mark the white skiff as it skims o'er the bay,
Or heedlessly bounds o'er the warrior's grave.

Oh, 'tis sweet to a heart unentangled and light,
When with hope's brilliant prospects the fancy is blest,
To pause 'mid its day–dreams so witchingly bright,
And mark the last sunbeams, while sinking to rest.

欢乐

克拉丽莎·斯科特·德莱尼[①]

欢乐犹如扬帆的风令我震颤，
如同喧哗的风
在伟岸的松林中谈笑怡然。
欢乐令我温暖
犹如太阳照在雨后的森林
荧光灿烂。

我纵情欢乐
——我大笑，我唱歌
我已在荒凉的路上走得太久，
在迷茫中苦苦思索
不知所措。

① 1901 ~ 1927，非裔诗人和社会工作者。生于亚拉巴马州塔斯基吉镇，韦尔斯利女子学院毕业，曾游历法国和德国。大学毕业后在华盛顿特区邓巴中学任教三年，并加入乔治娅·约翰逊组织的文学沙龙。婚后迁居纽约市，从事黑人儿童社会工作，不幸因肾病英年早逝。她出版了四部诗集，其作品不同凡响，是哈莱姆黑人文艺复兴运动的组成部分。作者在诗歌中并不探讨黑人具体的痛苦挣扎，常使用比兴手法描述自己的心路历程。

Joy

Clarissa Scott Delaney

Joy shakes me like the wind that lifts a sail,
Like the roistering wind
That laughs through stalwart pines.
It floods me like the sun
On rain–drenched trees
That flash with silver and green.

I abandon myself to joy—
I laugh—I sing.
Too long have I walked a desolate way,
Too long stumbled down a maze
Bewildered.

希望之鸟

艾米莉·狄金森[①]

希望是只羽毛丰满的鸟儿，
栖歇在我们的灵魂里，
唱着一首无词的歌，
从不中断停息。

那是狂风中能听到的最甜蜜的歌曲。
暴雨无情无义
令那只给众人温暖慰藉的小鸟
惊恐不已。

在陌生的海洋和寒冷的大地，
我曾听到它的优美旋律；
然而，无论如何艰难困苦，
它从未对我有任何索取。

---

① 1830～1886，生于马萨诸塞州阿默斯特镇一个书香世家，祖父是阿默斯特学院创建人之一。她从小聪颖敏慧，性格内向古怪，卓尔不群。大学只读了一年便辍学回家。长年身着白色衣裙，足不出户，养花种草，阅读写作，终身未婚，过着与世隔绝的生活。生前默默无闻，去世后其妹拉维尼亚将她日记中的近1800首诗歌整理出版，名声大噪，成为对美国诗歌发展具有重要影响力的人物。其作品短小精悍，语言风格极其鲜明，记录了她对美、大自然、社会和生死的独特思考与见解。

Hope Is the Thing with Feathers

Emily Dickinson

Hope is the thing with feathers
That perches in the soul,
And sings the tune without the words,
And never stops at all,

And sweetest in the gale is heard;
And sore must be the storm
That could abash the little bird
That kept so many warm.

I've heard it in the chillest land,
And on the strangest sea;
Yet, never, in extremity,
It asked a crumb of me.

潜力

艾米莉·狄金森

我们永远不会知道自己的潜力
　　直到我们发奋进取；
如果锲而不舍，
　　终可登峰造极。

我们传诵的英雄主义
　　将是凡人琐事；
假如我们勇往直前
　　成就最好的自己。

We Never Know How High We Are

Emily Dickinson

We never know how high we are
　　Till we are called to rise;
And then, if we are true to plan,
　　Our statures touch the skies—

The Heroism we recite
　　Would be a daily thing,
Did not ourselves the Cubits warp
　　For fear to be a King—

庄严

艾米莉·狄金森

那个我们已经结束的庄严仪式——
　　它仅仅是一场游戏，
或者阁楼里的一阵欣喜，
　　或者一个节日，

或者一次出门远行；或者往后，
　　与世长辞
我们已经明白，更妙的是
　　它会显露无遗。

That Is Solemn We Have Ended

Emily Dickinson

That is solemn we have ended,—
　　Be it but a play,
Or a glee among the garrets,
　　Or a holiday,

Or a leaving home; or later,
　　Parting with a world
We have understood, for better
　　Still it be unfurled.

七月问答

艾米莉·狄金森

七月，请回答
蜜蜂在哪？
羞晕在哪？
草垛在哪？

哦，七月说
——种子在哪？
花蕾在哪？
五月在哪？
请你回答我。

不，五月说
——让我看看白雪，
让我看看风铃，
让我看看松鸭！

松鸭争辩道
——玉米在哪？
雾霭在哪？
刺果在哪？
在这里——年度答。

Answer July

Emily Dickinson

Answer July
—Where is the Bee—
Where is the Blush—
Where is the Hay?

Ah, said July
—Where is the Seed
—Where is the Bud
—Where is the May
—Answer Thee—Me—

Nay—said the May—
Show me the Snow—
Show me the Bells—
Show me the Jay!

Quibbled the Jay—
Where be the Maize—
Where be the Haze—
Where be the Bur?
Here—said the Year—

伴侣

希尔达·杜里特尔[①]

只剩下我们俩 缄默冷淡：
我毫不隐瞒
憎恨和痛苦；
你急躁厌烦
抓住我的双手；
虽然没有用力，
却令我惴惴不安
犹如炭火旁
一只装着白色玫瑰的碗，
　　里面因受热低垂
　　但尚未枯萎的花瓣。

只剩下我们俩 惋惜悲叹：
犹如一堵空墙，野莽荒蛮
人们侃侃而谈，
夸耀他们的生活空间
优雅完善
但是两眼茫然
无知地以为
　　可以在那个空洞的世界
　　安息避难。

---

① 1886～1961，20世纪初叶先锋意象派代表人物之一。生于宾夕法尼亚州一个捷克移民家庭，在费城长大。其作品常借用希腊神话和自然景物来激发特定的个人情感。

只剩下我们俩 相依为伴：
我在脑海里
搜寻呐喊，
是什么奇迹
让我们相遇
在茫茫的人生绎站
　　荆棘丛生 风雨如磐，
　　我站在那里形孤影单？

We Two

Hilda Doolittle

We two are left:
I with small grace reveal
distaste and bitterness;
you with small patience
take my hands;
though effortless,
you scald their weight
as a bowl, lined with embers,
wherein droop
great petals of white rose,
forced by the heat
too soon to break.

We two are left:
as a blank wall, the world,
earth and the men who talk,
saying their space of life
is good and gracious,
with eyes blank

as that blank surface
their ignorance mistakes
for final shelter
and a resting–place.

We two remain:
yet by what miracle,
searching within the tangles of my brain,
I ask again,
have we two met within
this maze of dædal paths
in–wound mid grievous stone,
where once I stood alone?

埃瓦德妮

希尔达·杜里特尔

我，埃瓦德妮，
在阿波罗的嘴唇下，
第一次尝到了爱的甜蜜；
我的头发由鲜嫩的紫罗兰编织
或是山脊岩石上摇曳的
风信子；
我，埃瓦德妮，
是光明之神的伴侣。

他的蓬松秀发垂落在我的嘴里，
仿佛番红花的花瓣
拂面舒适，
犹如爱罗托斯河岸的
银色水芹沁人心脾；
他的嘴唇
在我的颏喉之间滑来滑去。

我的肩膀，
依然感到他刷子般的发丝，
我的双手被染成金色，
它们在那束黄花中，
魂牵梦萦如醉如痴。

Evadne

Hilda Doolittle

I first tasted under Apollo's lips,
love and love sweetness,
I, Evadne;
my hair is made of crisp violets
or hyacinth which the wind combs back
across some rock shelf;
I, Evadne,
was mate of the god of light.

His hair was crisp to my mouth,
as the flower of the crocus,
across my cheek,
cool as the silver–cress
on Erotos bank;
between my chin and throat,
his mouth slipped over and over.

Still between my arm and shoulder,
I feel the brush of his hair,
and my hands keep the gold they took,
as they wandered over and over,
that great arm–full of yellow flowers.

春雷

马克·范·多伦①

听，风寂静无声，
　　在黑夜的远方——
只见高原上一道闪电
　　正在疾驰狂奔。

室外温暖宜人，
　　在晴朗的夜空——
风暴的前沿
　　正在快步逼进。

树篱颤抖不停，
　　你也悚然失声。
但你是否听到
　　严冬的利刃轰然塌崩？

---

① 1894 ~ 1972，诗人和文学评论家，普利策奖获得者。生于伊利诺伊州一个农场，父亲是乡村医生。伊利诺伊大学毕业，并在哥伦比亚大学获文学博士学位。在哥伦比亚大学英文系从教40年，培养了不少作家和文学艺术人才。

Spring Thunder

Mark Van Doren

Listen. The wind is still,
　　And far away in the night—
See! The uplands fill
　　With a running light.

Open the doors. It is warm;
　　And where the sky was clear —
Look! The head of a storm
　　That marches here!

Come under the trembling hedge—
　　Fast, although you fumble… .
There! Did you hear the edge
　　Of winter crumble?

昨日和明天

保尔·劳伦斯·邓巴[①]

昨日我牵着你的手，
虔诚地、紧紧地牵着你的手。
我从心底里赞美它
以及它的委婉温柔。

但是今天我独自静坐，
充满悲伤、痛苦和酸楚。
难道我们爱情的黄金
必须放在火焰上锤炼不休？

昨日我曾和你一起行走，
多么甜蜜无忧。
生活犹如一首情歌，
没有结尾 只有开头。

啊，今天就像一首挽歌——
多想再用我的双臂拥抱你，
感受亲密的心动和喜悦，
如同初次与你相遇的时候。

① 1872～1906，19世纪末和20世纪初美国知名非裔诗人、小说家和剧作家。成长于俄亥俄州戴顿市，父母曾是肯塔基州黑奴。16岁开始在报刊上发表作品，其作品具有浓郁的南方黑人方言特色。

让我回溯曾经走过的路，
尽管曲折坎坷。
让我的心灵
忘却眼前所有的忧愁。

昨日激情似火，
今天悲痛如灸。
让我的灵魂停歇片刻，
然后踏上通往明天的道路。

Yesterday and To–morrow

Paul Laurence Dunbar

Yesterday I held your hand,
Reverently I pressed it,
And its gentle yieldingness
From my soul I blessed it.

But to–day I sit alone,
Sad and sore repining;
Must our gold forever know
Flames for the refining?

Yesterday I walked with you,
Could a day be sweeter?
Life was all a lyric song
Set to tricksy meter.

Ah, to–day is like a dirge,—
Place my arms around you,
Let me feel the same dear joy
As when first I found you.

Let me once retrace my steps,
From these roads unpleasant,
Let my heart and mind and soul
All ignore the present.

Yesterday the iron seared
And to–day means sorrow.
Pause, my soul, arise, arise,
Look where gleams the morrow.

希 望

爱丽丝·登巴-尼尔森[1]

狂涛汹涌的大海上，
一艘破损半沉的帆船即将失去最后一线希望；
一名男子拚命抓住桅杆，而风神波雷亚斯咆哮若狂，
　　遮住了月亮和星光，
　　这时蓦现一道闪电，将远方的海岸照亮。

Hope

Alice Dunbar-Nelson

Wild seas of tossing, writhing waves,
A wreck half-sinking in the tortuous gloom;
One man clings desperately, while Boreas raves,
　　And helps to blot the rays of moon and star,
　　Then comes a sudden flash of light, which gleams on shores afar.

① 1875 ~ 1935，新闻记者、专栏作家、政治活动家和女权运动倡导者。生于路易斯安那州新奥尔良市，是南北战争后在美国南方出生的第一代自由黑人。作为诗人，她是哈莱姆黑人文艺复兴运动的重要成员。

道别

爱丽丝·登巴·尼尔森

再见，亲爱的，再见；
在这离别的时刻，谁知道
　　我们是否还能会面
紧握双手
重温爱的誓言，
　　忘记悲伤，冰释前嫌。

亲爱的，失去你令我苦海无边。
也许，你会将我忘却；
但是，我的心会颤动
　　我记起我们一起度过的多年快乐时光
　　充满甜蜜的爱情和美好的留恋
　　悠远绵绵。

你回到家人的身边，
他们热情的拥抱和灿烂的笑脸。而留下我
　　独自呻吟哀怨；
为了你，我的爱，我的心动
我只好沿着灰暗乏味的生活路线
　　踽踽向前。

是的，你带走了炽热的爱。
我的生命中只剩下寒冷的冬天
　　枯燥，无聊，可怜；
为什么我还需努力生活和学习
保持微笑乐观，每天尝试
　　抹去心中对你的思念？

不，亲爱的，我宁愿躺下
昏睡沉眠；或者飞向遥远
　　那里没有残酷的命运，
有情人快乐地生活
　　运离沮丧，冷漠，阴险。

亲爱的，我不抱怨。
我只说，尊重再见。上帝保佑
　　我们见面的那一天；
也保佑你，我的爱与你同在
无论是悲伤的时刻或快乐的瞬间，
　　让你永远铭记我对你的思念。

Farewell

Alice Dunbar-Nelson

Farewell, sweetheart, and again farewell;
To day we part, and who can tell
　　If we shall e'er again
Meet, and with clasped hands
Renew our vows of love, and forget
　　The sad, dull pain.

Dear heart, 'tis bitter thus to lose thee
And think mayhap, you will forget me;
　　And yet, I thrill
As I remember long and happy days
Fraught with sweet love and pleasant memories
　　That linger still

You go to loved ones who will smile
And clasp you in their arms, and all the while
        I stay and moan
For you, my love, my heart and strive
To gather up life's dull, gray thread
        And walk alone.

Aye, with you love the red and gold
Goes from my life, and leaves it cold
        And dull and bare,
Why should I strive to live and learn
And smile and jest, and daily try
        You from my heart to tare?

Nay, sweetheart, rather would I lie
Me down, and sleep for aye; or fly
        To regions far
Where cruel Fate is not and lovers live
Nor feel the grim, cold hand of Destiny
        Their way to bar.

I murmur not, dear love, I only say
Again farewell. God bless the day
        On which we met,
And bless you too, my love, and be with you
In sorrow or in happiness, nor let you
        E'er me forget.

思 维

爱丽丝 · 登巴 · 尼尔森

一条敏捷，连续的事物链，
进进出出，万花筒一般闪现，
时而直泻，时而在荒野的涡流中盘旋，
没有秩序，也没有规律驱动，
但是它们总是不停地迅速伸延。

Thought

Alice Dunbar-Nelson

A swift, successive chain of things,
That flash, kaleidoscope-like, now in, now out,
Now straight, now eddying in wild rings,
No order, neither law, compels their moves,
But endless, constant, always swiftly roves.

紫罗兰

爱丽丝·登巴·尼尔森

我已好久没有想到紫罗兰，
含羞在脚下绽开的野生草桂花瓣。
在沉醉的四月，情人云雨巫山
在原野中流连忘返；
紫罗兰令人想到娇艳的花亭，
还有蝴蝶结和胸针，以及透着香水味的精致纸巾；
装模作样的花花公子，炫目的霓虹灯
令人麻木的葡萄酒和夜总会的歌舞厅。
我的思绪游离真正的甜美如此遥远，
以至忘了广袤原野和溪流清泉
上帝创造的完美化身——
含羞的野生紫罗兰和梦幻般的极乐园。
如今——无意之中，你使我想起
紫罗兰，以及我的灵魂中那丝已被忘却的光线。

Violets

Alice Dunbar–Nelson

I had no thought of violets of late,
The wild, shy kind that spring beneath your feet
In wistful April days, when lovers mate
And wander through the fields in raptures sweet.;
The thought of violets meant florists' shops,
And bows and pins, and perfumed papers fine;
And garish lights, and mincing little fops
And cabarets and songs, and deadening wine.
So far from sweet real things my thoughts had strayed,
I had forgot wide fields, and clear brown treams The perfect loveliness that God has made,—
Wild violets shy and Heaven–mounting dreams.
And now—unwittingly, you've made me dream
Of violets, and my soul's forgotten gleam.

九月又至

杰西·雷德蒙·佛塞特[1]

九月又至!
仿佛那么离奇
未曾发誓的我却坐在这里
对着金色的秋天伤感追忆——

最深切渴望的一声叹息,
灿烂的容颜和坚定无比的山盟海誓,
对狂热亲吻的
敏捷反应和立即投诚屈膝!

那就是我!
九月又至!
仿佛那么离奇
信守诺言的我却心力交瘁独坐于此
默默祈祷将一切忘记!

① 1882 ~ 1961,中学教师、诗人和小说家。生于新泽西州一个黑人牧师家庭,康乃尔大学毕业。其文学作品真实描述了1920年代美国黑人的生活状态,为美国黑人文学的诞生奠定了基础。

Again It Is September

Jessie Redmon Fauset

Again it is September!
It seems so strange that I who made no vows
Should sit here desolate this golden weather
And wistfully remember—

A sigh of deepest yearning,
A glowing look and words that knew no bounds,
A swift response, an instant glad surrender
To kisses wild and burning!

Ay me!
Again it is September!
It seems so strange that I who kept those vows
Should sit here lone, and spent, and mutely praying
That I may not remember!

甜蜜的回忆

杰西·雷德蒙·佛塞特

总是这样，夜幕降临
　　暮色苍茫，
我忘却眼前的烦恼惆怅
　　去寻找记忆模糊的过去印象。
我进入一个早被遗忘的梦境，
　　仿佛回到往日时光，
直到突然到达春天的心脏——
　　春天带来了我的情郎！
我又看见那条木板铺就的小径，
　　树林中洒满了金色的月光。
我听到倦鸟的轻声鸣唱
　　在沉醉的微风中进入梦乡；
我牵着你的手，凝视你的双眼，
　　我亲吻你的嘴唇，——哦，甜蜜盖世无双！
哦，记忆战胜了时空与死亡！
　　哦，片刻美妙时光！

Douce Souvenance

Jessie Redmon Fauset

Again, as always, when the shadows fall,
In that sweet space between the dark and day,
I leave the present and its fretful claims
And seek the dim past where my memories stay.
I dream an old, forgotten, far–off dream,
And think old thoughts and live old scenes anew,
Till suddenly I reach the heart of Spring—
The spring that brought me you!
I see again a little woody lane,
The moonlight rifting golden through the trees;
I hear the plaintive chirp of drowsy bird
Lulled dreamward by a tender, vagrant breeze;
I hold your hand, I look into your eyes,
I touch your lips,—oh, peerless, matchless dower!
Oh, Memory thwarting Time and Space and Death!
Oh, Little Perfect Hour!

前行

卡丽·罗·摩根·费格斯[①]

我们正在前行，真正地前行
　　难道你听不到我们的脚步声？
我们披荆斩棘
　　我们无往不胜。

我们有约伯一样的耐心，
　　我们像约书亚一样走过险径
像所罗门一样，我们建造了庙宇。
　　像亚伯拉罕一样，我们对上帝信仰虔诚。

在财富和商业的大街上，
　　我们正在抗议游行
我们一步一步前进，创造历史
　　为了我们自己和我们的子孙。

我们建起了学校和教堂，
　　我们完成了我们的历史使命。
我们从奴隶的小屋出发
　　走进了立法大厅。

弟兄们，难道你不精神振奋？
　　快加入我们的行列，不要做局外人
因为我们正在抗议游行，是的，我们在前进
　　伴着时代的歌声。

---

① 1878 ~ 1968，黑人女教师、诗人和剧作家，生于佐治亚州。其作品谴责种族主义，呼唤黑人为民权和社会公平正义奋起抗争，以及赞颂黑人对美国社会进步的贡献。她的作品为哈莱姆黑人文艺复兴运动的兴起奠定了基础。

我们在前进，稳步前进
　　架接鸿沟，跨越溪流
攀登进步的山峰
　　到达我们最美的梦境。

我们正在前行，真正地前行
　　难道你听不到我们的脚步声？
我们披荆斩棘
　　我们无往不胜。

We Are Marching

Carrie Law Morgan Figgs

We are marching, truly marching
　　Can't you hear the sound of feet?
We are fearing no impediment
　　We have never known defeat.

Like Job of old we have had patience,
　　Like Joshua, dangerous roads we've trod
Like Solomon we have built out temples.
　　Like Abraham we've had faith in God.

Up the streets of wealth and commerce,
　　We are marching one by one
We are marching, making history,
　　For ourselves and those to come.

We have planted schools and churches,
　　We have answered duty's call.
We have marched from slavery's cabin

To the legislative hall.

Brethren can't you catch the spirit?
You who are out just get in line
Because we are marching, yes we are marching
To the music of the time.

We are marching, steady marching
Bridging chasms, crossing streams
Marching up the hill of progress
Realizing our fondest dreams.

We are marching, truly marching
Can't you hear the sound of feet?
We are fearing no impediment
We shall never know defeat.

黑女王

卡丽·罗·摩根·费格斯

致敬！这位诚实的黑人姑娘，
　　让我们起立鼓掌；
献上国际皇冠，
　　加冕她为世界女王。

她是窈窕淑女的榜样，
　　她亭亭玉立娴静端庄，
远远在平均身高之上，
　　她是当之无愧的女王。

她四处奔忙，
　　恪尽职守勇于担当；
你们所有人，无论伟大渺小，
　　请加冕她为世界女王。

她挺直地站在她的男人身旁，
　　决不会让他们倒下受伤，
为她的勇敢敬礼，
　　然后加冕她为世界女王。

The Black Queen

Carrie Law Morgan Figgs

All hail! This honest dusky maid,
Let all others prostrate fall;
Bring forth the international diadem,
And crown her queen of all.

In all pure womanly qualities,
She stands serene and tall,
Way up above the average,
This makes her queen of all.

She's not a sluggard at any place,
She answers duty's call
Come all ye people, small and great,
And crown her queen of all.

She stands bolt upright by her men,
She will not let them fall,
Now for her valor, tip your hat,
And crown her queen of all.

人生

卡丽·罗·摩根·费格斯

1.
片刻的喜悦欢欣，
　　然后一个小时的痛苦呻吟，
一天的阳光明媚，
　　然后一周的梅雨浇淋，
半旬的和平，
　　然后一个月的纷争，
所有这些交织一起
　　便组成了人生。

2.
一名挚友，
　　十几个敌人，
两扇敞开的大门，
　　二十个闭门羹，
鸿运的交椅，
　　逆境的刀刃；
这些朋友和对手
　　构成了我的人生。

3.
破晓时的花蕾，
　　晌午间的玫瑰，
黄昏时衰败，
　　到了夜晚已经枯萎。
困惑的轰鸣，
　　横笛的悲催，

如此这般
　　筑成了人生的路轨。

4.
一个微笑，随之一滴泪水，
　　像一枚神秘的珍珠翡翠，
稍作停留，便冲入
　　疯狂的对垒，
刚刚还在亲吻，接着却是刺毁
　　来自判徒的图谋不轨；
我想你会认同
　　这就是生命的真伪。

Life

Carrie Law Morgan Figgs

1
A moment of pleasure,
　　An hour of pain,
A day of sunshine,
　　A week of rain,
A fortnight of peace,
　　A month of strife,
These taken together
　　Make up life.

2
One real friend
　　To a dozen foes,
Two open gates,

’Gainst twenty that’s closed,
Prosperity’s chair,
Then adversity’s knife;
These my friends
Make up life.

3
At daybreak a blossom,
At noontime a rose,
At twilight ’tis withered,
At evening ’tis closed.
The din of confusion,
The strain of the fife,
These with other things
Make up life.

4
A smile, then a tear,
Like a mystic pearl,
A pause, then a rush
Into the mad whirl,
A kiss, then a stab
From a traitor’s knife;
I think that you’ll agree with me,
That this life.

远方的歌

约翰·古尔德·弗莱彻[①]

无论清醒或昏睡，
　　我无法长久安卧：
从我的窗扉
　　飘来一首远方的歌。

歌声犹如微风吹动的银铃
　　婉转缠绵，
悦耳动听，
　　在空中飘荡悠远：

那首歌充满了疲惫与悲伤，
　　却没有任何颓废与挫败：
它在生命的长河中回荡
　　从古至今直到未来。

它的力量无法用语言描述，
　　我不能将它从未来带到这里，
到那时，人们的灵魂会复苏
　　庆祝勇敢战胜恐惧。

① 1886 ~ 1950，意象派诗歌代表人物之一，第一位获普利策奖的南方诗人。生长于阿肯色州小石城，曾就读哈佛大学，辍学后曾在英国生活多年。因罹患抑郁症在小石城一个池塘投水自杀。为纪念这位杰出诗人，阿肯色州将其公共图书馆系统一个分馆以约翰·古尔德·弗莱彻命名。

我被那些朦胧甜蜜的诗句
　　一次又一次欺骗，
反复的失败未能教会我停止
　　追求无用的韵律音旋。

那遥远的音乐，不言而喻
　　全是我的错：
我不该捕捉毁弃，
　　一首远方的歌。

A Distant Song

John Gould Fletcher

Whether awake or sleeping,
　　I cannot rest for long:
By my casement comes creeping
　　A distant song.

A song like the chiming of silver
　　Bells which the breezes play,
Seeming to float for ever
　　Towards an unseen day:

A song that is weary with sorrow,
　　Yet knows not any defeat:
Through the past, through to-day, through to-morrow,
　　It echoes on life's long street.

Could I but make words of its power,
        Bring it from the future here,
Men's souls would be waking, that hour,
        To the victory against fear.

But the vague sweet stanza befools me
        With its calm joy, time after time,
And no failure here ever schools me
        To cease from an idle rhyme.

That music afar, unspoken,
        'Tis I have done it wrong:
I caught, and I have broken,
        A distant song.

为谁

玛丽·韦斯顿·福特汉姆①

夜空星光闪闪
　　犹如璀璨的皇冠，
柔和的月光
　　将大地映射得色彩斑澜；
秋风穿过山岭草地
　　轻轻哀叹，
夏日时光越来越短，
　　流浪的人儿，你是否会想念我和我的温暖？

你的生活充满快乐，
　　你的家庭幸福美满，
没有一个人眉宇间流露抑郁寡欢，
　　没有一个人胸怀中装着忐忑不安——
黄昏时分，
　　你在炉火旁逍遥舒坦，
想想那个在痛苦中挣扎的人吧，
　　亲爱的，请为我祈祷平安。

如果在黑色的悲伤中哀叹，
　　你的脸颊失色灰暗，
在你最痛苦的时刻，
　　亲爱的，我将与你一同悲泣肠断。
虽然夜晚沉寂黑暗，
　　时间于你过得太慢，

---

① 1843～1905，黑人学校教师，生于南卡罗来纳州一个黑人牧师家庭。其诗歌描绘了美国内战后南方黑人家庭的生活状态，探讨有关母性、情感、道德、死亡和宗教方面的主题。

但我将轻声说："不必悲伤；
　　我会为你祈求爱的仙丹。"

我知道，将来
　　我可能会珍惜尘世的虚渺；
我知道，出于本能的爱
　　仍然需要呵护善待。
虽然大海可能会将
　　你我分开，
但这颗永恒的心
　　绝不停止对你的思念和爱。

For Who?

Mary Weston Fordham

When the heavens with stars are gleaming
　　Like a diadem of light,
And the moon's pale rays are streaming,
　　Decking earth with radiance bright;
When the autumn's winds are sighing,
　　O'er the hill and o'er the lea,
When the summer time is dying,
　　Wanderer, wilt thou think of me?

When thy life is crowned with gladness,
　　And thy home with love is blest,
Not one brow o'ercast with sadness,
　　Not one bosom of unrest—
When at eventide reclining,
　　At thy hearthstone gay and free,

Think of one whose life is pining,
Breathe thou, love, a prayer for me.

Should dark sorrows make thee languish,
Cause thy cheek to lose its hue,
In the hour of deepest anguish,
Darling, then I'll grieve with you.
Though the night be dark and dreary,
And it seemeth long to thee,
I would whisper, "be not weary;"
I would pray love, then, for thee.

Well I know that in the future,
I may cherish naught of earth;
Well I know that love needs nurture,
And it is of heavenly birth.
But though ocean waves may sever
I from thee, and thee from me,
Still this constant heart will never,
Never cease to think of thee.

五月致四月

菲利普·弗伦诺[1]

没有你的阵雨，我无法孕育花蕾，
　　每一片土地都是贫瘠的废墟；
如果你不哭泣，我的繁花仍在沉睡，
　　它们是如此享受你的泪滴。

你的消亡为五月创造了机运，
　　所以我必须放弃我的一切：
我的和煦微风，我的浓绿树林
　　它们的甜美即将面临骄阳的炽热！

我用我的浓荫覆盖逝去的四月：
　　我的霓裳是她赠予——
春季三姊妹中，我的职责
　　是在某天结束我们的胜利：

这样，大自然的一切归于安眠；
　　岁月千古：
时光飞逝，五月终结春天，
　　夏季在她的坟墓上欢乐起舞！

---

① 1752～1832，诗人、辩论家、航海家和报纸编辑。生于纽约市一个葡萄酒商人家庭，新泽西学院（即现普林斯顿大学）毕业。在美国独立战争时期，发表了一系列反对英王的政论文章，被誉为美国革命诗人。其诗歌作品结合新古典主义和浪漫主义风格，对美国浪漫派诗歌和自然诗歌的发展产生了深远影响。

May to April

Philip Freneau

Without your showers, I breed no flowers,
Each field a barren waste appears;
If you don't weep, my blossoms sleep,
They take such pleasures in your tears.

As your decay made room for May,
So I must part with all that's mine:
My balmy breeze, my blooming trees
To torrid suns their sweets resign!

O'er April dead, my shades I spread:
To her I owe my dress so gay—
Of daughters three, it falls on me
To close our triumphs on one day:

Thus, to repose, all Nature goes;
Month after month must find its doom:
Time on the wing, May ends the Spring,
And Summer dances on her tomb!

渴望

安吉丽娜·韦尔德·克里姆克[1]

月亮潜隐的天际有一丝金色的彩晕；
透过浮云，只有一两颗星星；
树叶呢喃细语，柔润恬静，
哦！对你的渴望令我泣不成声。

The Want of You

Angelina Weld Grimké

A hint of gold where the moon will be;
Through the flocking clouds just a star or two;
Leaf sounds, soft and wet and hushed,
And oh! the crying want of you.

① 1880 ~ 1958，生于波士顿一个多元文化家庭，母亲是白人，父亲有一半黑人血统。毕业于韦斯理女子学院，曾在华盛顿特区和纽约任中学英文教师，同时从事写作。她创作的诗歌和戏剧集中探讨种族问题，揭露对黑人的歧视和暴力，是哈莱姆黑人文艺复兴运动的重要组成部分。

冬日暮光

安吉丽娜·韦尔德·克里姆克

寂静如死神般在周围游荡，
却被轻声的叹息驱逐无处隐藏；
几棵削瘦、赤裸、冰寒的大树，
在蓝色的天空下掠影浮光；
一条小路通向玉米花絮曾在的地方；
一棵冷杉形孤影只坚毅刚强；
垂挂在冷杉的远空，
是一颗我曾经喜爱的星星，那时田野尚未枯黄。

A Winter Twilight

Angelina Weld Grimké

A silence slipping around like death,
Yet chased by a whisper, a sigh, a breath;
One group of trees, lean, naked and cold,
Inking their cress ‘gainst a sky green–gold;
One path that knows where the corn flowers were;
Lonely, apart, unyielding, one fir;
And over it softly leaning down,
One star that I loved ere the fields went brown.

小小灰色的梦想

安吉丽娜·韦尔德·克里姆克

小小灰色的梦想，
我坐在大海旁
灰色的大海旁，
将你们放在我的膝盖上。

我送你们下海出航，
　　一个接着一个，
　　小小灰色的梦想，
在灰色的云层下，
驶进灰色的海洋，
你们扬帆起航，
从我空空的膝盖上，
　　小小灰色的梦想。

起航！起航！
驶向黑色的海洋，
水天相接的地方。

Little Grey Dreams

Angelina Weld Grimké

Little grey dreams,
I sit at the ocean's edge,
At the grey ocean's edge,
With you in my lap.

I launch you, one by one,
        And one by one,
        Little grey dreams,
Under the grey, grey, clouds,
Out on the grey, grey, sea,
You go sailing away,
From my empty lap,
        Little grey dreams.

Sailing! Sailing!
Into the black,
At the horizon's edge.

黑指

安吉丽娜·韦尔德·克里姆克

我刚刚看见一件至美的东西，
　　恬静纤细，
　　一棵笔直的落羽翠柏，
　　映衬在金色的天幕里，
　　灵敏，
　　精致，
　　犹如指向天空的
　　黑色手指。
美丽恬静的手指，你为什么是黑色？
你为什么指向天际？

The Black Finger

Angelina Weld Grimké

I have just seen a most beautiful thing,
　　Slim and still,
　　Against a gold, gold sky,
　　A straight black cypress,
　　Sensitive,
　　Exquisite,
　　A black finger
　　Pointing upwards.
Why, beautiful still finger, are you black?
And why are you pointing upwards?

春晓

安吉丽娜·韦尔德·克里姆克

我目睹黎明来到，
　　春天的黎明来到。
红日喷薄而出
　　穿过淡紫色的薄雾，
穿过灰云，穿过碧霄。
多么宁静！多么美好！
　　一只醒来欢唱的小鸟，
展翅飞向太阳，转眼变成一片黑影，
　　歌声在远方缭绕。
我尽情张开双臂，
　　迎接阳光普照，
　　脸上洋溢着欢笑。
啊！活着多好，爱着多好，
　　在黎明，
　　在春晓。

At the Spring Dawn

Angelina Weld Grimké

I watched the dawn come,
	Watched the spring dawn come.
And the red sun shouldered his way up
	Through the grey, through the blue,
Through the lilac mists.
The quiet of it! The goodness of it!
	And one bird awoke, sang, whirred
A blur of moving black against the sun,
	Sang again—afar off.
And I stretched my arms to the redness of the sun,
	Stretched to my finger tips,
	And I laughed.
Ah! It is good to be alive, good to love,
At the dawn,
	At the spring dawn.

寂静之前

黑兹尔·霍尔①

我会想到睡莲
在一个褐色的水池中生息繁衍，
我的呼吸犹如溪流一样悠闲，
我的双手变得凉爽柔软。

仿佛我独自等待
在一个木制的空间；
我会模仿百合
在宁静之中沉潜。

如果思念的阵痛突现，
如果渴望随风翩跹，
我会将它当作一片树叶的阴影
飘过我的面前。

① 1886～1924，生于明尼苏达州圣保罗市，幼年随父母迁居俄勒冈州波特兰市。12 岁因伤病致下肢瘫痪，辍学在家，学习缝纫，以手工制作婚礼服和童装为生，同时从事写作。其作品描述她窗户之外的大自然变化以及她缝纫制衣时的感想。诗集《窗帘》获 1921 年度诗歌杂志青年诗人奖。

Before Quiet

Hazel Hall

I will think of water–lilies
Growing in a darkened pool,
And my breath shall move like water,
And my hands be limp and cool.

It shall be as though I waited
In a wooden place alone;
I will learn the peace of lilies
And will take it for my own.

If a twinge of thought, if yearning
Come like wind into this place,
I will bear it like the shadow
Of a leaf across my face.

乐天派

J.W. 哈蒙德[①]

谁不愿看到蓝色的天空
　　或绿色的草丛?
或夏天盛开的鲜花
　　姹紫嫣红?

阳光让人赏心悦目——
　　而凄寂的雨声
会使人泪如泉涌,
　　消解灵魂的伤痛。

哦,这个世界古老恢弘!
　　我爱每一个季节的变化无穷,
清澈优雅的河水溪流,
　　以及峡谷山峰。

我的生命悄然临终,
　　我的双脚不会糟践草皮花丛,
虽然尘世充满美丽,
　　与神同在的天堂更加绚丽兴荣!

---

① 生卒年月不详。自学成才的非裔女诗人,未受过正规学校教育。诗歌作品发表在其生活的内布拉斯加州奥马哈市的报刊上。

The Optimist

J. W. Hammond

Who would have the sky any color but blue,
Or the grass any color but green?
Or the flowers that bloom the summer through
Of other color or sheen?

How the sunshine gladdens the human heart—
How the sound of the falling rain
Will cause the tender tears to start,
And free the soul from pain.

Oh, this old world is a great old place!
And I love each season's change,
The river, the brook of purling grace,
The valley, the mountain range.

And when I am called to quit this life,
My feet will not spurn the sod,
Though I leave this world with its beauty rife,—
There's a glorious one with God!

为民而歌

弗朗西丝·艾伦·沃特金斯·哈珀[1]

让我为民众作曲歌唱，
　　让歌声温暖老人和孩子的心房；
让歌声唤醒世界，
　　犹如战斗的号角激越嘹亮。

不是为了兵刃相向，
　　不是为了凶残争强；
而是为了让歌声震撼心灵
　　使生命更加丰盛兴旺。

让我为疲惫的人们歌唱，
　　让他们忘却生活的烦恼紧张，
直到焦虑的眉头舒展，
　　和愁苦的心情快畅。

让我为幼儿歌唱，
　　为他们指引方向，
让充满爱与责任的歌声，
　　在他们的人生旅途中飘荡。

---

① 1825 ~ 1911，生于马里兰州巴尔的摩市，3 岁时丧失父母，由身为牧师的叔父抚养长大。13 岁在一个开书店的白人家庭当保姆，利用工作之余学习阅读和写作，成为一名教师和多产的非裔女诗人，并终身致力于废除奴隶制和争取妇女参政权利。

我会为穷困孤寡老人歌唱，
　　阴影遮住了他们的目光；
愿他们生活在明亮宁静的广厦，
　　没有黑夜的地方。

我们的世界如此痛苦凄凉，
　　需要音乐的纯净明朗，
去平息悲嚎怒吼的
　　嘈杂声响。

让音乐抚慰所有的悲伤，
　　直到战争与罪恶消亡；
人心变得温柔善良
　　世界充满和平之光。

Songs for the People

Frances Ellen Watkins Harper

Let me make the songs for the people,
　　Songs for the old and young;
Songs to stir like a battle-cry
　　Wherever they are sung.

Not for the clashing of sabres,
　　For carnage nor for strife;
But songs to thrill the hearts of men
　　With more abundant life.

Let me make the songs for the weary,
　　Amid life's fever and fret,

Till hearts shall relax their tension,
And careworn brows forget.

Let me sing for little children,
Before their footsteps stray,
Sweet anthems of love and duty,
To float o'er life's highway.

I would sing for the poor and aged,
When shadows dim their sight;
Of the bright and restful mansions,
Where there shall be no night.

Our world, so worn and weary,
Needs music, pure and strong,
To hush the jangle and discords
Of sorrow, pain, and wrong.

Music to soothe all its sorrow,
Till war and crime shall cease;
And the hearts of men grown tender
Girdle the world with peace.

思 乡

弗朗西丝·艾伦·沃特金斯·哈珀

哦，让我走吧，我已倦怠，
我的头灼热难耐，
我渴望闻到故乡的空气，
将之吸入每条燃烧的静脉。

我渴望再次见到我的故乡，
在那遥远的群山之外。
聆听潺潺溪流的音符，
感受神清气爽的畅快。

我的家位于深深的山坳，
周围常年白雪皑皑。
溪流轻言细语，
瀑布飞溅欢快。

在那里，我的疲惫和渴望
将被欢乐和温暖化解。
在那里，岩石和高山松林
与湛蓝的天空同在。

我知道你的景色多么秀丽，
我的母亲曾在那里祈祷膜拜。
她的窄床虽然低矮，
但我宁愿死于床下与她一同掩埋。

因为我知道她将与我紧紧相依，
倾诉对我的思念和爱。

我的姊妹们将唱起
那些熟悉动听的歌谣曲牌。

她们会抚摸我滚烫的额眉，
犹如离别时的表白。
然后将我临终的长榻
装扮成洁白的花海。

哦，让我走吧，我已倦怠，
我的头灼热难耐，
我渴望闻到故乡的空气，
将之吸入每条燃烧的静脉。

Yearnings for Home

Frances Ellen Watkins Harper

Oh let me go I’m weary here
And fevers scorch my brain,
I long to feel my native air
Breathe o’er each burning vein.

I long once more to see
My home among the distant hills,
To breathe amid the melody
Of murmering brooks and rills.

My home is where eternal snow
Round threat’ning craters sleep,
Where streamlets murmer soft and low
And playful cascades leap.

Tis where glad scenes shall meet
My weary, longing eye;
Where rocks and Alpine forests greet
The bright cerulean sky.

Your scenes are bright I know,
But there my mother pray'd,
Her cot is lowly, but I go
To die beneath its shade.

For, Oh I know she'll cling
'Round me her treasur'd long,
My sisters too will sing
Each lov'd familiar song.

They'll soothe my fever'd brow,
As in departed hours,
And spread around my dying couch
The brightest, fairest flowers.

Then let me go I'm weary here
And fevers scorch my brain,
I long to feel my native air,
Breathe o'er each burning vein.

故 土

弗朗西丝·艾伦·沃特金斯·哈珀

上帝保佑我们的故土，
　　那里不再有枷锁与黑奴，
哦，愿她从此代表
　　真理和自由。

上帝保佑我们的故土，
　　那里埋葬着我们逝去的先祖，
让你统率的和平之光
　　照耀他们的坟墓。

上帝扶助我们的故土，
　　终止那里的一切冲突，
从你的手中得到阵雨的浇灌，
　　生活更加美好富足。

上帝保佑我们的故土，
　　庇护那里的家园和母幼
哦，愿她永远高昂
　　真理和正义之首。

God Bless Our Native Land

Frances Ellen Watkins Harper

God bless our native land,
    Land of the newly free,
Oh may she ever stand
    For truth and liberty.

God bless our native land,
    Where sleep our kindred dead,
Let peace at thy command
    Above their graves be shed.

God help our native land,
    Bring surcease to her strife,
And shower from thy hand
    A more abundant life.

God bless our native land,
    Her homes and children bless,
Oh may she ever stand
    For truth and righteousness.

葬我于自由的土地

弗朗西丝·艾伦·沃特金斯·哈珀

无论你将我埋葬在哪里，
低洼平原，或山丘高地；
无论坟墓多么简陋，
但那里绝对不能存在奴隶。
我不能安息，如果在坟墓周围
我听到奴隶的脚步颤抖不止；
他映在墓碑上的身影
会使墓地变得恐怖悲戚。
我不能安息，如果我听到
一群戴着枷锁的奴隶蹒跚走向末日，
母亲撕心裂肺的绝望哀嚎
犹如诅咒在颤抖的空气中升起。
我无法入眠，如果我看到皮鞭
抽打在她身上并浸透了伤口的血渍，
将她的婴儿从她的怀中夺去，
犹如离开母巢的雏鸟充满恐惧。
我会发抖战栗，如果我听到
猎犬追逐撕咬逃跑的奴隶，
当被重新套上可憎的铁链时
被俘者的徒劳哀乞。
如果我看到母亲臂膀中的青春少女
被标价出售交易，
我的眼睛会闪现悲愤的火焰，
我的惨白脸颊将涨红羞泣。
亲爱的朋友，我将安息
如果那里没有弱肉强食；
我将在任何坟墓安息

如果没有人将他的兄弟当作奴隶。
我不要高傲的纪念碑
去吸引路人的注意；
我的灵魂唯一渴望的是
葬我于一片自由的土地。

Bury Me in a Free Land

Frances Ellen Watkins Harper

Make me a grave where'er you will,
In a lowly plain, or a lofty hill;
Make it among earth's humblest graves,
But not in a land where men are slaves.
I could not rest if around my grave
I heard the steps of a trembling slave;
His shadow above my silent tomb
Would make it a place of fearful gloom.
I could not rest if I heard the tread
Of a coffle gang to the shambles led,
And the mother's shriek of wild despair
Rise like a curse on the trembling air.
I could not sleep if I saw the lash
Drinking her blood at each fearful gash,
And I saw her babes torn from her breast,
Like trembling doves from their parent nest.
I'd shudder and start if I heard the bay
Of bloodhounds seizing their human prey,
And I heard the captive plead in vain
As they bound afresh his galling chain.

If I saw young girls from their mother's arms
Bartered and sold for their youthful charms,
My eye would flash with a mournful flame,
My death–paled cheek grow red with shame.
I would sleep, dear friends, where bloated might
Can rob no man of his dearest right;
My rest shall be calm in any grave
Where none can call his brother a slave.
I ask no monument, proud and high,
To arrest the gaze of the passers–by;
All that my yearning spirit craves,
Is bury me not in a land of slaves.

鱼贩

马斯登·哈特利[①]

我从月亮的脸上
采集银币，
我用蓝鸟的翅膀制成鳍翼。
我用树荫中的李子当作眼睛，
我从阳光下的桃唇上取来胭脂。
我用这些材料为你做了一条天堂鱼，
将它放游在初秋的天空里。
我坐在溪流岸边
惊奇地发现
芳草已现枯黄的痕迹。
你是否认为从彩虹里来的鱼
依然美丽？
它们为谁而制？
为谁我将它们
放游天际？

① 1877～1943，现代派画家和诗人，生于缅因州。曾在欧洲学习和生活多年，其绘画和诗歌深受巴黎和柏林立体派艺术影响。

Fishmonger

Marsden Hartley

I have taken scales from off
The cheeks of the moon.
I have made fins from bluejays' wings,
I have made eyes from damsons in the shadow.
I have taken flushes from the peachlips in the sun.
From all these I have made a fish of heaven for you,
Set it swimming on a young October sky.
I sit on the bank of the stream and watch
The grasses in amazement
As they turn to ashy gold.
Are the fishes from the rainbow
Still beautiful to you,
For whom they are made,
For whom I have set them,
Swimming?

夜曲

卡尔·贞吉·哈特曼[①]

在寂静的海湾
  夜晚的梦变得温柔迷茫，
    海浪消失在宝石般的沙滩，
    犹如往日失去的希望。

夜晚的梦变得温柔迷茫
  在夏天色彩斑斓的大海，
    犹如往日失去的希望，
    海鸥的歌声在微风中徘徊。

在夏日色彩斑斓的大海
  帆船闪烁着幽灵般的白光魔影，
    海鸥的歌声在微风中徘徊
    在单调的黑夜里消失殆尽。

帆船闪烁着幽灵般的白光魔影，
  它们来回漂游，
    在单调的黑夜里消失殆尽，
    就像夏日的海市蜃楼。

① 1867 ~ 1944，生于日本长崎，母亲是日本人，父亲是德国商人。出生不久其母病故，随父迁居德国，15 岁移民美国，1894 年成为美国公民。他是摄影和艺术评论家及著名的无政府主义者，是最早将日本俳句介绍给美国读者的诗人之一。其诗歌作品深受象征主义和东方文学影响。

它们来回漂游
　犹如起伏跌宕的恋情，
　　夏日的海市蜃楼
　　我们永远无法重复的梦境。

犹如起伏跌宕的恋情
　星辰的黎明将帆船逐个照亮，
　　就像我们永远无法重复的梦境；
　　海鸥依然循踪飞翔。

星辰的黎明将帆船逐个照亮
　虽然前途昏暗未卜，
　　海鸥依然循踪飞翔
　　寻觅它们的梦境之处。

为了寻觅它们的的梦境之处，
　那个遥远寂静的海湾，
　　它们迷失方向前途未卜，
　　海浪消失在宝石般的沙滩
　　夜晚的梦温柔迷茫，
　　犹如往日失去的希望。

Nocturne

Carl Sadakichi Hartmann

The dreams of night fall soft and gray
    Upon the summer–colored seas,
        Like some lost hope of yesterday,
        The sea–mew's song is on the breeze.

Upon the summer–colored seas
    Sails gleam and glimmer ghostly white,
        The sea–mew's song is on the breeze
        Lost in the monotone of night.

Sails gleam and glimmer ghostly white,
    They come and slowly drift away,
        Lost in the monotone of night,
        Like visions of a summer–day.

They shift and slowly drift away
    Like lovers' lays that wax and wane,
        The visions of a summer–day
        Whose dreams we ne'er will dream again.

Like lovers' lays wax and wane
    The star dawn shifts from sail to sail,
        Like dreams we ne'er will dream again;
        The sea–mews follow on their trail.

The star dawn shifts from sail to sail,
As they drift to the dim unknown,
The sea–mews follow on their trail
In quest of some dreamland zone.

In quest of some far dreamland zone,
Of some far silent sea–swept land,
They are lost in the dim unknown,
Where waves fade on jeweled sand
And dreams of night fall soft and gray,
Like some lost hope of yesterday.

为何爱你

卡尔·贞吉·哈特曼

我为何爱你?
　　请问海风为何四处游荡,
海滨为何充满了潮汐,
月亮为何漫步于天堂;
就像远航的船只
行进在阴沉寂静的海面;
　　海鸟为何在海滨翱翔展翅
　　那里海浪轻声吟唱入眠
　　星光映照着沙滩婀娜的身姿!

Why I Love Thee?

Carl Sadakichi Hartmann

Why I love thee?
　　Ask why the seawind wanders,
Why the shore is aflush with the tide,
Why the moon through heaven meanders;
Like seafaring ships that ride
On a sullen, motionless deep;
　　Why the seabirds are fluttering the strand
　　Where the waves sing themselves to sleep
　　And starshine lives in the curves of the sand!

爱情问答

瓦尔特·埃弗瑞特·霍金斯[1]

亲爱的，问我为什么我爱你，
　　那么我将问玫瑰
为什么它爱早春的露滴
　　冬季刚刚离去；
为什么好奇的蜜蜂
　　爱花蕊的甘汁？
如果它们回答我，
　　我将乐意回答你。

亲爱的，问我为什么我爱你，
　　那么我将问鲜花
为什么它喜欢阳光灿烂的夏日，
　　或夏天阵雨的淋浴；
我将会问情人的心
　　它为什么爱明月，
或星星闪烁的天际
　　在六月的黑夜里？

① 1888～？，黑人，曾当过邮递员，生长于北卡罗来纳州。1920年发表诗集《和谐与争吵》。

亲爱的，问我为什么我爱你，
那么我将问藤蔓
为什么它的卷须毫无顾虑
攀缘缠绕橡树的身躯；
为什么你爱芬芳的木樨
胜于野草蒺藜？
只要你回答我，
我将一定回答你。

亲爱的，问我为什么我爱你，
请让云雀回答你，
为什么它的心里充满歌声
当暮色临近时；
为什么情人不再叹息
如果她的爱是真情实意？
只要你回答我，
我将一定回答你。

Ask Me Why I Love You

Walter Everette Hawkins

Ask me why I love you, dear,
And I will ask the rose
Why it loves the dews of Spring
At the Winter's close;
Why the blossoms' nectared sweets
Loved by questing bee,—
I will gladly answer you,
If they answer me.

Ask me why I love you, dear,
        And I will ask the flower
Why it loves the Summer sun,
        Or the Summer shower;
I will ask the lover's heart
        Why it loves the moon,
Or the star–besprinkled skies
        In a night in June.

Ask me why I love you, dear,
        I will ask the vine
Why its tendrils trustingly
        Round the oak entwine;
Why you love the mignonette
        Better than the rue,—
If you will but answer me,
        I will answer you.

Ask me why I love you, dear,
        Let the lark reply,
Why his heart is full of song
        When the twilight's nigh;
Why the lover heaves a sigh
        When her heart is true;
If you will but answer me,
        I will answer you.

昏睡的世界

瓦尔特·埃弗瑞特·霍金斯

一朵花在山林里开放，
一首歌在林间的溪流中回荡；
小花开过便会凋零，
无人听到小溪的声音，
　　因为世界仍在昏睡不醒。

月光透过窗帘
照在一个熟睡婴儿的床缘；
带有酒窝的小脸上闪过一阵呓语和笑意，
除了天使却没有人能捕捉到它们的美丽，
　　因为昏睡的世界仍然沉浸在梦里。

一只小鸟在玉米地里欢唱，
一朵玫瑰在荆棘丛下绽放；
但玫瑰的芬芳和小鸟的歌声
在晨风中消散得无踪无影
　　世界仍在沉睡不醒。

沉睡的旧世界变得越来越苍老无力，
最甜蜜的欢乐渐渐消逝；
如果像黎明那样能激发灵感的美景只是时间的玩偶——
它们闪现之后便荡然无存，
　　世界继续昏睡不醒。

The Drowsy World Dreams On

Walter Everette Hawkins

A flower bloomed out on a woodland hill,
A song rose up from the woodland rill;
But the floweret bloomed but to wither away,
And no man heard what the stream had to say,
For the drowsy world dreamed on.

Thro the frills of a curtain a moonbeam crept,
Till it fell on the crib where a nursling slept;
And a whisper and smile lit a wee dimpled face,
But none save the angels their beauty could trace,
For the drowsy world dreamed on.

A wee bird piped out mid the corn,
A rose bloomed out beneath the thorn;
But the scent of the rose and the birdling's lay
On the winds of the morning were wafted away
While the drowsy world dreamed on.

And the drowsy old world's growing gloomy and gray,
While the joys that are sweetest are passing away;
And the charms that inspire like the picture of dawn
Are but playthings of Time—they gleam and are gone,
While the drowsy world dreams on.

雨过天晴

约瑟芬·D. 赫德[1]

来吧，威尔，让我们重归于好，
　　请忘记我们的过错，
因为语言只能带来无谓的痛苦，
　　何必为此郁闷烦恼。

请抛开那些无中生有的荒谬，
　　让我们永远不给忧伤让道。
生活中应该充满欢乐的歌声，
　　哪有时间用来欺骗争吵。

我将尽力克制狂怒气恼，
　　并且停止频繁的哭闹；
路上一定会有荆棘杂草，
　　让我们一起清除拔掉。

我们怎能像一对蠢鸟，
　　为一封信发怒狂躁；
时间是如此宝贵，
　　我们必须做得更好。

① 1861～1921，生于北卡罗来纳州，父母皆为奴隶，南北战争后获自由。曾在多所中小学担任教师，1890 年出版诗集《早晨的荣耀》。其作品致力于激励黑人青年。

Sunshine After Cloud

Josephine D. Heard

Come, "Will," let's be good friends again,
Our wrongs let's be forgetting,
For words bring only useless pain,
So wherefore then be fretting.

Let's lay aside imagined wrongs,
And ne'er give way to grieving,
Life should be filled with joyous songs,
No time left for deceiving.

I'll try and not give way to wrath,
Nor be so often crying;
There must some thorns be in our path,
Let's move them now by trying.

How, like a foolish pair were we,
To fume about a letter;
Time is so precious, you and me;
Must spend ours doing better.

平安夜

艾拉·希金森[①]

划过一团薄雾霭云
　　落日犹如一个猩红的火轮
像一块猫眼石燃烧在海面
　　那里曾是钢铁般寒冷。

带着炫丽的紫红黄金，
　　你将归来于明天的黎明……
哦，太阳，你却永远不能带回
　　已经流逝的圣诞时辰。

Christmas Eve

Ella Higginson

Straight thro' a fold of purple mist
　　The sun goes down—a crimson wheel—
And like an opal burns the sea
　　That once was cold as steel.

With pomp of purple, gold and red,
　　Thou wilt come back at morrow's dawn…
But thou can'st never bring, O Sun,
　　The Christmas that is gone!

① 1861 ~ 1940，生于堪萨斯州，4 岁随父母迁居俄勒冈州。14 岁起在报刊上发表诗歌，生前共发表 6 部诗集和 100 部短篇小说，作品多以美国西北部邻近太平洋地区为背景。

假期结束

莱斯利·平克尼·希尔[①]

从容光焕发的迷人魅力，
从梦想期待的日子开始，
从辽阔世界带来的欢喜
从高山和小溪，
带着古铜肤色，敏捷肢体
神经兴奋，头脑清晰，
我们再次迅速投入
为了生计的搏击。
分配任务的指令
简单严厉。
那个暴君冷酷专制，
对我们的言行无情评判抨击。
但是那些短暂假日
留下光辉记忆。
而欢乐，无论怎样的代价，
永远不会完全失去。
因为我们带着某种美感，
和对生命更加公正的认识，
去面对那些无尽的职责，
艰苦劳作和冲突争执。

---

① 1880～1960，黑人教育家和作家，生于弗吉尼亚州，中学时随父母迁居新泽西州，哈佛大学毕业，哈莱姆黑人文艺复兴运动成员之一。

Vacation End

Leslie Pinckney Hill

From the charm of radiant faces,
From the days we took to dream,
From the joy of open spaces,
From the mountain and the stream,
Bronzed of sunlight, nerves a–tingle,
Keen of limb and clear of head,
Speed we back again to mingle
In the battle for our bread.
Now again the stern commanding
Of the chosen task is heard,
And the tyrant, care, is standing
Arbiter of deed and word.
But the radiance is not ended,
And the joy, whate'er the cost,
Which those fleeting days attended
Never can be wholly lost.
For we bring to waiting duty,
To the labor and the strife,
Something of the sense of beauty,
And a fairer view of life.

忏悔（读 W.E.B. 杜波依斯的《黑水》有感）

伊丽莎白·柯蒂斯·霍尔曼[1]

我没有思考……我不知道……
　　我给的理由是多么苍白枯槁
回应我的黑人兄弟
　　长期所受的虐待和痛苦煎熬！

在他无言而耐心的灵魂中，
　　也许我的冷漠轻藐，
使他的命运阴影更加深重
　　更加漫长的黑夜，更加昏暗的世道。

我已经读了一篇令人燃烧的书稿，
　　刺眼的光芒在鞭打灵魂的火焰中闪耀，
我将不再助纣为虐
　　让我的良知沉默睡觉。

对于我以前没有注意的所有非公道，
　　因为出生机遇我的生活优越美好，
我请求黑人兄弟的宽恕和原谅
　　并为他的需要而呼叫！

---

① 1879 ~？，诗人和剧作家，生于康涅狄格州，长年受精神疾患困扰，对遭受歧视和不公正待遇的黑人群体充满同情。

After a Reading of "Darkwater"

Elizabeth Curtis Holman

I did not think...I did not know...
What pale excuse is this I make
In answer to my brother's woe,
Age–long, for deep injustice sake!

Across his mute and patient soul,
While I have gone my heedless way,
The shadows of a fate might roll
That deepened night and darkened day.

But I have read a burning page,
That glowed with white and soul–wrung fire,
And now no more I may engage
My conscience with a feeble hire.

For all the wrong I did not heed,
Chance–born in happier paths to live,
I cry unto my brother's need
One word of love and shame...forgive!

情侣

伊丽莎白·柯蒂斯·霍尔曼

夏日我们摘了一朵玫瑰
　　在情侣门旁，
我们的欢笑是如此陶醉，
　　夜幕迟迟没有下降。

转眼一年已近尾声！
　　树篱赤条精光——
有道是即使热恋也会变冷，
　　所以如今只有迷迭香。

We Pulled a Rose in Summer Time

Elizabeth Curtis Holman

We pulled a rose in summer time
　　Beside True Lover's Gate,
Our lips sent up so sweet a chime,
　　That twilight lingered late:

Now look how is the year grown old! —
　　How leafless hedge and tree, —
'Tis said that even love grows cold,
　　So here is rosemary.

自由与奴隶

乔治·摩西·霍尔顿[①]

唉！难道我生而为奴，
终身戴着枷锁？
只有艰辛痛苦的劳作，
没有任何欢乐？

我在束缚中挣扎已久
渴望获得自由！
唉！我必须不断申诉——
为了被剥夺的自由。

天啊！你为什么不拯救
这个无声的坟墓——
减轻一个奴隶的痛苦，
缓解他的悲伤和酸楚？

快来吧，自由，让你欢乐的声音
响彻我的两只被皮鞭打烂的耳朵！
快来吧，自由，让欢乐淹没我的悲伤
驱散我的恐惧和颤抖。

① 1798 ~ 1883，奴隶，生于北卡罗来纳州，曾被农场主多次转卖，直到 1865 年才获自由，被誉为北卡罗来纳州游吟诗人。1829 年其诗集《自由的希望》出版，是美国历史上第一部由奴隶出版的著作。

对邪恶的暴君说，住手，
压迫实在肮脏下流。
让和平成为快乐的主宰
而不是受欺压的家奴。

让那只戴着锁链的和平鸽，
在天空中展翅遨游。
它用非洲丛林的音喉，
为自由咕咕呼唤不休。

哦，自由！为了你，
人们常常头破血流。
你是神圣的太阳，
自然之神赐予我们的最高奖酬。

告别奴隶制的丑陋，
以及野蛮的恶毒。
我憎恨看到自己
被奴役的悲伤耻辱。

亲爱的自由之神！我渴望躺在你的胸口
尽情呼吸自由；
就像回巢的天鹅，
在你的笑容中找到归宿。

哦，圣洁的避难所——天堂般舒适温柔！
我要逃离奴役冤仇——
在你的庇护下躲过风暴，
获得自由！

On Liberty and Slavery

George Moses Horton

Alas! and am I born for this,
To wear this slavish chain?
Deprived of all created bliss,
Through hardship, toil and pain!

How long have I in bondage lain,
And languished to be free!
Alas! and must I still complain—
Deprived of liberty.

Oh, Heaven! and is there no relief
This side the silent grave—
To soothe the pain—to quell the grief
And anguish of a slave?

Come Liberty, thou cheerful sound,
Roll through my ravished ears!
Come, let my grief in joys be drowned,
And drive away my fears.

Say unto foul oppression, Cease:
Ye tyrants rage no more,
And let the joyful trump of peace,
Now bid the vassal soar.

Soar on the pinions of that dove
Which long has cooed for thee,
And breathed her notes from Afric's grove,
The sound of Liberty.

Oh, Liberty! thou golden prize,
So often sought by blood—
We crave thy sacred sun to rise,
The gift of nature's God!

Bid Slavery hide her haggard face,
And barbarism fly:
I scorn to see the sad disgrace
In which enslaved I lie.

Dear Liberty! upon thy breast,
I languish to respire;
And like the Swan unto her nest,
I'd like to thy smiles retire.

Oh, blest asylum—heavenly balm!
Unto thy boughs I flee—
And in thy shades the storm shall calm,
With songs of Liberty!

办公楼

海伦·霍伊特[1]

我们在大楼入口亲吻，
在那幢建筑物巨大冰凉的石门
将你吞噬之前。
我们在花岗岩拱门下亲吻。
然后你转身离去不见踪影
四周和头顶都是坚硬高耸的墙壁
带着巨石可怕的重量和无情。
但是在那一刻它们对我们非常仁慈
用双臂将我们紧紧重叠在一起
当我们亲吻时。

The Office Building

Helen Hoyt

We kissed there in the stone entrance,
In the great cool stone mouth of the building,
Before it took you.
We kissed under the granite arches.
And then you turned and were gone
And high about and above were the hard towered walls,
The terrible weights of stone, relentless,
But for the moment they had been kind to us,
Folding us with arms
While we kissed.

---

① 1887 ~ 1972，生于康涅狄格州，毕业于巴纳德女子学院，曾任诗歌杂志编辑 20 余年，并创作出版了 4 部诗集，较著名的作品包括《艾丽丝公园》（*Ellis Park*）、《记忆》（*Memory*）、《灯杆》（*Lamp Posts*）和《夜雨》（*Rain at Night*）。

我的人民

郎斯敦·休斯[1]

歌唱梦想的人，
演讲故事的人，
天生的舞者，
在命运面前放声大笑的人——
那就是我的人民。
洗碗盘的帮工，
开电梯的男童，
投骰子的赌徒，
女士的仆佣，
厨师，
侍从，
爵士乐手，
婴儿护工，
船舶装卸工，
港口搬运工，
美发师，
杂耍滑稽演员，
以及马戏团乐队员工——
都是歌唱家，
都是演说家。
舞者——
我的天！多么具有天赋的舞者！
歌手——
我的上帝！多么神奇美妙的歌手！

---

① 1902 ~ 1967，诗人、小说家、剧作家和社会活动家，生于密苏里州，在美国中西部地区不同城镇长大，高中毕业后前往纽约，曾就读哥伦比亚大学。开创了爵士诗歌流派，是哈莱姆黑人文艺复兴运动领导人之一。

歌手和舞者，
舞者和无忧者。
无忧者？是的，欢笑……欢笑……欢笑——
永远笑对命运的人们。

My People

Langston Hughes

Dream-singers,
Story-tellers,
Dancers,
Loud laughers in the hands of Fate—
My People.
Dish-washers,
Elevator-boys,
Ladies' maids,
Crap-shooters,
Cooks,
Waiters,
Jazzers,
Nurses of babies,
Loaders of ships,
Porters,
Hairdressers,
Comedians in vaudeville
And band-men in circuses—
Dream-singers all,
Story-tellers all.
Dancers—
God! What dancers!
Singers—

God! What singers!
Singers and dancers,
Dancers and laughers.
Laughers?
Yes, laughers...laughers...laughers—
Loud–mouthed laughers in the hands of Fate.

我之爱

郎斯敦·休斯

我爱看到银色的大月亮，
　　在天上闪着光芒；
我爱见到璀璨的小星星，
　　乌云消失在远方。

我爱夜晚的雨滴
　　落在房顶上的声响；
我爱微风的轻叹，
　　在黎明前的曙光。

我爱湛蓝的深邃，
　　在我上帝的天堂；
但是我认为，与所有这些相比，
　　我更爱我热恋的姑娘。

My Loves

Langston Hughes

I love to see the big white moon,
    A–shining in the sky;
I love to see the little stars,
    When the shadow clouds go by.

I love the rain drops falling
    On my roof–top in the night;
I love the soft wind's sighing,
    Before the dawn's gray light.

I love the deepness of the blue,
    In my Lord's heaven above;
But better than all these things I think,
    I love my lady love.

我们的土地

郎斯敦·休斯

我们应该拥有一片光明的土地，
那里的阳光灿烂美丽，
我们应该拥有一片芬芳的的土地
那里的暮色是一块由玫瑰和黄金
织成的柔软手绢彩饰，
而不是这片土地
生命冷漠无情无义。

我们应该拥有一片葱绿的土地，
那里的树林高大茂密，
低垂的枝头上鹦鹉呢喃细语，
炫丽如日，
而不是这片土地，鸟儿灰暗无声无息。

呵，我们应该拥有一片欢乐的土地，
一片充满了慈爱喜悦美酒和歌声的土地，
而不是这片土地，罪恶横行乌烟瘴气。

Our Land

Langston Hughes

We should have a land of sun,
Of gorgeous sun,
And a land of fragrant water
Where the twilight is a soft bandanna handkerchief
Of rose and gold,
And not this land
Where life is cold.

We should have a land of trees,
Of tall thick trees,
Bowed down with chattering parrots
Brilliant as the day,
And not this land where birds are gray.

Ah, we should have a land of joy,
Of love and joy and wine and song,
And not this land where joy is wrong.

分合

海伦·杰克逊[①]

Ⅰ.分
在同一屋檐下，
他们终日以礼相待。
一起接受永恒的忠告，
不愠不火 且慢且快。
出于礼貌，也出于无奈，
尽管身心疲惫 欢乐不在
那颗勇敢的心仍然保持微笑，
试图将痛苦掩盖
还有无望，追念与悲哀。
以殉道者的坚强
自我忍耐。
用苦涩的红色神香草
减轻饥渴的残害。
哦，多么勇敢坚强的心！
上帝将所有的日子分开，
欢乐只在约定的时辰到来。

Ⅱ.合
无声无息之中，
广袤的大陆与大海
试图将他们分开。
可是为时已晚！
有情人终于相爱。

① 1830～1885，出生于马萨诸塞州阿默斯特镇，是艾米莉·狄金森的同学和朋友，毕生致力于争取和保护印地安人权益。其小说《雷蒙娜》描述了美国西南部印地安人的生活遭遇，至今已重印三百余次。

有什么比空气更轻?
有什么比光更快?
太阳之下有何意外?
光，空气和太阳不可侵害。
他们保持永恒
彼此交融的存在。
在庄严的圣礼中，
他们忠贞相爱。
痛苦的命运
无法将他们分开。

Two

Helen Hunt Jackson

Ⅰ. Apart

One place—one roof—one name—their daily bread
In daily sacrament they break
Together, and together take
Perpetual counsel, such as use has fed
The habit of, in words which make
No lie. For courtesy's sweet sake
And pity's, one brave heart whose joy is dead,
Smiles ever, answering words which wake
But weariness; hides all its ache,—
Its hopeless ache, its longing and its dread;
Strong as a martyr at the stake
Renouncing self; striving to slake
The pangs of thirst on bitter hyssop red
With vinegar! O brave, strong heart!

God sets all days, all hours apart,
Joy cometh at his hour appointed.

Ⅱ . Together

No touch—no sight—no sound—wide continents
And seas clasp hands to seperate
Them from each other now. Too late!
Triumphant Love has leagued the elements
To do their will. Hath light a mate
For swiftness? Can it overweight
The air? Or doth the sun know accidents?
The light, the air, the sun, inviolate
For them, do constant keep and state
Message of their ineffable contents
And raptures, each in each. So great
Their bliss of loving, even fate
In parting them, hath found no instruments
Whose bitter pain insatiate
Doth kill it, or their faith abate
In presence of Love's hourly sacraments.

十月的夜晚

罗宾逊·杰夫斯[①]

薄雾中船舶的笛鸣雄浑低沉，
岸边的花岗岩似乎颤抖不停。
郊狼对着山谷回应，
溪流边枯草中的小狼爪
被秋天的初雨浸润，
它们起伏不平的哀嚎惊动高空中的星星。
什么星星？金牛座中紧密相连的七姊妹星。
猎户星即将升起，
我为夏天逝去而庆幸，
天空渐渐变得黑暗空旷，湿润宁静。

October Evening

Robinson Jeffers

Male-throated under the shallow sea-fog
Moaned a ship's horn quivering the shorelong granite.
Coyotes toward the valley made answer,
Their little wolf-pads in the dead grass by the stream
Wet with the young season's first rain,
Their jagged wail trespassing among the steep stars.
What stars? Aldebaran under the dove-leash Pleiades.
I though, in an hour Orion will be risen,
Be glad for summer is dead and the sky
Turns over to darkness, good storms, few guests, glad rivers.

---

① 1887 ~ 1961，环境保护运动先驱，生于宾夕法尼亚州一个传教士家庭，其文学作品主要以加尼福利亚中部太平洋海岸为背景，用史诗般的风格描绘大自然的美丽。

石与鹰

罗宾逊·杰夫斯

这是一个符号象征
许多高明悲催的思想
注视着它们自己的眼睛。

这块灰石，高高耸立
在岬角，那里海风凛冽
不容树木生息，

地震作证，风暴签名：
在岩石的顶端
栖歇着一只猎鹰。

我想，这就是你的徽章
挂在未来的天空；
不是十字架，也不是蜂房，

而是这个形象；光明的力量，黑暗的静谧；
强烈的意识与终极的漠视
结合在一起；

生伴随着安静的死；猎鹰的
现实主义眼睛和行为
融汇于

岩石的无穷神秘，
不被失败击倒
不为成功骄傲。

Rock and Hawk

Robinson Jeffers

Here is a symbol in which
Many high tragic thoughts
Watch their own eyes.

This gray rock, standing tall
On the headland, where the seawind
Lets no tree grow,

Earthquake–proved, and signatured
By ages of storms: on its peak
A falcon has perched.

I think, here is your emblem
To hang in the future sky;
Not the cross, not the hive,

But this; bright power, dark peace;
Fierce consciousness joined with final
Disinterestedness;

Life with calm death; the falcon's
Realist eyes and act
Married to the massive

Mysticism of stone,
Which failure cannot cast down
Nor success make proud.

今昔

查尔斯·伯特伦·约翰逊[1]

“人生由一首歌组成”
　　我曾吟唱在少年的清晨；
快接近山顶时
　　响起悦耳的回声。

长着翅膀的韶华
　　转眼飞翔到已近正午的青春，
“人生由一首歌组成”
　　我唱着走向战争。

唉，我的双脚已经走到
　　生命的黄昏。
我同样不会错过
　　这段充满希望和恐惧的旅程。

嘹亮的青春之歌
　　充满燃烧的激情。
但它只是叮当之声——
　　犹如铜钹的空鸣。

如今，我歌唱我的爱人，
　　带着一颗笃定明智的心，
“人生全部由爱筑成，
　　而歌只是其中一部分。”

---

① 1880 ~ 1958，黑人教师、牧师。生于密苏里州，毕业于芝加哥大学，3 部诗集的作者。

Now and Then

Charles Bertram Johnson

"All life is built from song"
In youth's young morn I sang;
And from a top–near hill
The echo broke and rang.

The years with pinions swift
To youth's high noon made flight,
"All life is built from song"
I sang amid the fight.

To life's sun–setting years,
My feet have come—Alas!
And through its hopes and fears
Again I shall not pass.

The lusty song my youth
With high–heart ardor sang
Is but a tinkling sound—
A cymbal's empty clang.

And now I sing, my Dear,
With wisdom's wiser heart,
"All life is built from love,
And song is but a part."

希望之歌

查尔斯·伯特伦·约翰逊

时辰已过晨旦，
　　我仍卧床辗转；
乌云笼罩空中，
　　草坪抑郁寡欢；
我有歌声相伴
　　直到阴霾消散。

时辰已是正午，
　　不见月弓月盘；
空中雨水如注，
　　草坪蒙受摧残；
我有歌声相伴
　　直到阴霾消散。

时辰已近黄昏，
　　信仰不需推断；
天空乌云密布，
　　世界一遍昏暗；
我有歌声相伴
　　直到阳光灿烂。

A Song of Hope

Charles Bertram Johnson

Day is at the gate,
　　I am risen late;
Clouds laze in the air,
　　Clouds sleep on the grass;
I have song to spare
　　Till the shadows pass.

Day is at the noon,
　　No thread of bow or moon;
Rain is in the air,
　　Drenched and limp the grass;
I have song to spare
　　Till the shadows pass.

Day is at the close,
　　Faith no logic knows;
Rain–clouds blur the air,
　　All the world is dun;
I have song to spare
　　Till to–morrow's sun.

雪

查尔斯·伯特伦·约翰逊

整天云块
　　变冷降落，
柔软的白絮覆盖
　　原野山河；
现在我明白
　　为什么雪会到来：
平卧的赤裸黑色土地
　　与天空紧紧相依。

Snow

Charles Bertram Johnson

All day the clouds
    Grow cold and fall,
And soft the white fleece shrouds
    Field, hill and wall;
And now I know
    Why comes the snow:
The bare black places lie
    Too near the sky.

神奇

芬顿·约翰逊[①]

虽然我被囚禁在监狱的壁垒，
我的灵魂随着无忧的溪流漫游迂回
穿过镶嵌着金色雏菊的绿色原野，
还有骑士般的水仙花和向日葵。
附近有个棕色眼瞳的男孩在玩耍，
一个上天恩赐的可爱小宝贝。
“哦，小朋友，”我恳求道。
“请给我一朵花，让我的孤独牢房有所点缀。”
他摘了一朵蒲公英，
那种丑陋的花卉，
将它轻轻放进我的手里。
在他的眼眸中，我看见了爱的至美，
顿时蒲公英变成了玫瑰。

① 1888 ~ 1958，诗人、小说家、杂志编辑和哈莱姆黑人文艺复兴运动早期成员，生于芝加哥一个黑人中产阶级家庭，父亲是铁路搬运工。他曾就读西北大学、芝加哥大学和哥伦比亚大学。其诗歌作品以反映黑人痛苦心路历程著称。

The Miracle

Fenton Johnson

Though I was dwelling in a prison house,
My soul was wandering by the carefree stream
Through fields of green with gold eyed daisies strewn,
And daffodils and sunflower cavaliers.
And near me played a little browneyed child,
A winsome creature God alone conceived,
"Oh, little friend," I begged. "Give me a flower
That I might bear it to my lonely cell."
He plucked a dandelion, an ugly bloom,
But tenderly he placed it in my hand,
And in his eyes I saw the sign of love.
'Twas then the dandelion became a rose.

幻想

芬顿·约翰逊

1.
我是星光，
我是月光，
在我生命的黎明破晓之前，
我是晚霞夕阳。
我是小河
逶迤流淌
追寻紫色的梦想，
我是嫩绿三月
明媚的春光，
我是金色歌鸲
优美的鸣唱——
　　我是爱的宝藏。

2.
我是晨光，
我是暮光，
在我出生之前，
我是所有飞禽的
婉转吟唱。
我是花季少女的
羞红脸庞，
我是勤奋少年的
坚毅目光，
我是夏日的骄阳，
我是秋天的金黄，
我是四季之美——
　　我是爱的宝藏。

Revery

Fenton Johnson

1.
I was the starlight
I was the moonlight
I was the sunset,
Before the dawning
        Of my life;
I was the river
Forever winding
To purple dreaming,
I was the glowing
Of youthful Springtime,
I was the singing
Of golden songbirds,—
        I was love.

2.
I was the sunlight,
I was the twilight,
I was the humming
Of winged creatures
        Ere my birth;
I was the blushing
Of lily maiden,
I was the vision
Of youthful striving,
I was the summer,
I was the autumn,
I was the All–time—
        I was love.

统治者

芬顿·约翰逊

据说在混乱的欧洲，许多国王会为了享乐一天而倾其所有。

我见过一名君主将快乐的珠宝紧握在手。

在费城的伦巴德大街上，当夜幕降临地球的时候，我凝视着一个比无月的天空还要漆黑的工友。他坐在面粉袋堆成的宝座上，旁若无人挥舞着他的手，伴随两个小男孩用吉他弹奏的雷格泰姆节奏。

上帝保佑统治费城伦巴德街的诸侯。

Rulers

Fenton Johnson

It is said that many a king in troubled Europe would sell his crown for a day of happiness.

I have seen a monarch who held tightly the jewel of happiness.

On Lombard street in Philadelphia, as evening dropped to earth, I gazed upon a laborer duskier than a sky devoid of moon. He was seated on a throne of flour bags, waving his hand imperiously as two small boys played on their guitars the ragtime tunes of the day.

God's blessing on the monarch who rules on Lombard Street in Philadelphia.

祝福

乔治娅·道格拉斯·约翰逊[①]

勇往直前，我的儿子，
愿你鹏程万里！
伟大的成就，虽然未知，
正等着
你的努力。
可惜我不能
与你同行，
我已完成我的朝圣之旅。
但是生活在召唤你！
志存高远，我的儿子，
新的一天已经开始，
锦绣前程通过奋斗才能获取！

---

① 1880 ~ 1966，美国最早的黑人女性剧作家和作曲家之一，生于亚特兰大一个多元文化家庭，母亲具有非裔和印地安人血统，父亲是黑人和英格兰人混血后代。毕业于亚特兰大大学，30 岁开始写诗，出版 4 部诗集，是哈莱姆黑人文艺复兴运动重要成员。

Benediction

Georgia Douglas Johnson

Go forth, my son,
Winged by my heart's desire!
Great reaches, yet unknown,
Await
For your possession.
I may not, if I would,
Retrace the way with you,
My pilgrimage is through,
But life is calling you!
Fare high and far, my son,
A new day has begun,
Thy star–ways must be won!

永恒的美丽

詹姆斯·韦尔顿·约翰逊[①]

遭到人生风暴的打击，
忍受生活痛苦的经历，
只有你的臂膀给我扶持，
只有你的胸膛给我慰藉。

在人生旅途中，磨难来袭，
日月失辉　昏天黑地；
见到你可爱的双眸中闪烁的镇定光芒，
我便感到称心如意。

于我而言，世界上所有的一切
都被环抱于你的双臂；
在你的眸瞳光影中，
我看见唯一永恒的美丽。

---

① 1871 ~ 1938，著名民权运动活动家和作家，美国有色人种协进会早期重要领导人。生于乔治亚州，亚特兰大大学毕业。其诗歌在哈莱姆黑人文艺复兴时期声誉卓著。诗歌《放声歌唱》被谱曲后称为美国黑人国歌，传唱至今。20世纪初叶曾被西奥多·罗斯福总统任命出使委内瑞拉和尼加拉瓜，1934年成为纽约大学首位黑人教授。

Beauty That Is Never Old

James Weldon Johnson

When buffeted and beaten by life's storms,
When by the bitter cares of life oppressed,
I want no surer haven than your arms,
I want no sweeter heaven than your breast.

When over my life's way there falls the blight
Of sunless days, and nights of starless skies;
Enough for me, the calm and steadfast light
That softly shines within your loving eyes.

The world, for me, and all the world can hold
Is circled by your arms; for me there lies,
Within the lights and shadows of your eyes,
The only beauty that is never old.

感觉

詹姆斯·韦尔顿·约翰逊

似乎星星没有那么明亮，
太阳失去了光芒，
我心烦意乱，
　　感觉你已去了远方。

仿佛天空没有那么蔚蓝晴朗，
事事都要你帮忙，
我不知所措，
　　感觉你已去了远方。

宛若万物错乱无章，
每一天都是那么漫长，
连小鸟也忘了歌唱，
　　感觉你已去了远方。

好像只能叹息惆怅，
眼泪汪汪，
我口干舌燥，
　　感觉你已去了远方。

Sence You Went Away

James Weldon Johnson

Seems lak to me de stars don't shine so bright,
Seems lak to me de sun done loss his light,
Seems lak to me der's nothin' goin' right,
　　Sence you went away.

Seems lak to me de sky ain't half so blue,
Seems lak to me dat ev'ything wants you,
Seems lak to me I don't know what to do,
　　Sence you went away.

Seems lake to me dat ev'ything is wrong,
Seems lak to me de day's jes twice es long,
Seems lak to me de bird's forgot his song,
　　Sence you went away.

Seems lak to me I jes can't he'p but sigh,
Seems lak to me ma th'oat keeps gettin' dry,
Seems lak to me a tear stays in ma eye,
　　Sence you went away.

放声歌唱

詹姆斯·韦尔顿·约翰逊

放开每一个嗓门歌唱，
直到地球和天堂
充满自由和谐的音响；
让我们欢乐的歌声高高飘扬
在九天云霄之上，
让它像汹湧的大海一样响亮。
唱一首充满信仰的歌，黑暗的过去教给我们的信仰，
唱一首充满希望的歌，光明的今天带给我们的希望；
面对崭新一天的朝阳，
让我们继续前进直到胜利在望。

我们曾爬涉过险峻的山岗，
忍受残酷的皮鞭棍棒，
在绝望中挣扎彷徨；
踏着坚定的步伐，
难道我们疲惫的双脚
没有来到我们祖先曾经叹息的地方？
我们走过一条被泪水洗涮的路，
我们闯过一道被鲜血浸透的岗，
走出过去的压抑悲伤
我们现在终于站起来
站在一个星光明亮的地方。

见证我们疲惫岁月的上苍，
目睹我们无声流泪的神灵，
是你带领我们走在漫长的征途上。
你的强大力量

指引我们走进希望之光。
我们祈祷，让我们永远走在正道上。
永不偏离我们最初遇见你的地方，
唯恐我们的心灵被尘世的美酒灌醉，
将你忘却而迷失方向。
愿我们永远站立
虔诚祷告上帝，
忠心热爱家乡。

Lift Ev'ry Voice and Sing

James Weldon Johnson

Lift ev'ry voice and sing,
'Til earth and heaven ring,
Ring with the harmonies of Liberty;
Let our rejoicing rise
High as the list'ning skies,
Let it resound loud as the rolling sea.
Sing a song full of the faith that the dark past has taught us,
Sing a song full of the hope that the present has brought us;
Facing the rising sun of our new day begun,
Let us march on 'til victory is won.

Stony the road we trod,
Bitter the chastening rod,
Felt in the days when hope unborn had died;
Yet with a steady beat,
Have not our weary feet
Come to the place for which our fathers sighed?
We have come over a way that with tears has been watered,
We have come, treading our path through the blood of the slaughtered,

Out from the gloomy past,
  'Til now we stand at last
Where the white gleam of our bright star is cast.

God of our weary years,
God of our silent tears,
Thou who has brought us thus far on the way;
Thou who has by Thy might
Led us into the light,
Keep us forever in the path, we pray.
Lest our feet stray from the places, our God, where we met Thee,
Lest, our hearts drunk with the wine of the world, we forget Thee;
Shadowed beneath Thy hand,
May we forever stand,
True to our God,
True to our native land.

我见到了你

约书亚·亨利·小琼斯[①]

我昨晚路过时见到了你，
　　你的身影镶嵌在金色的天幕上；
透过快速隐退的阳光
　　你犹如一位年长的女王，
你的微笑是黑暗世界的
　　一道光芒。
我的灵魂里有一首歌在回荡——
　　百灵鸟的歌声婉转悠扬。

我昨晚路过时见到了你，
　　你的长发闪耀着金光，
你的眼中流露出一道
　　明快友善的光芒。
我边走边唱
　　直到黑夜茫茫。
但是我的心里亮如白昼，
　　百灵鸟的歌声余音绕梁。

① ？～1955，1920年代美国较知名非裔诗人。生于南卡罗来纳州，出版《四季》《世界之心》和《法律制裁》三部诗集。

I Saw You

Joshua Henry Jones, Jr.

I saw you as I passed last night,
    Framed in a sky of gold;
And through the sun's fast paling light
    You seemed a queen of old,
Whose smile was light to all the world
    Against the crowding dark.
And in my soul a song there purled—
    Re–echoed by the lark.

I saw you as I passed last night,
    Your tresses burnished gold,
While in your eyes a happy bright
    Gleam of your friendship told.
And I went singing on my way;
    On, on into the dark.
But in my heart still shone the day,
    And still—still sang the lark.

愿望

约书亚·亨利·小琼斯

你的欢乐无比甜蜜
　　你的心中无忧无虑；
你的悲伤转瞬即逝，
　　爱神，请想念我一会儿。

生活晦暗无趣；
　　我不求你将我铭记
你的希望仅是寒冷过去
　　留下的灰烬遗迹。

悲伤是如此沉重凄迷
　　不能长久存留在记忆里。
友情的最大奖赏
　　莫过于幸福的回忆。

玫瑰的清香浸弥于
　　暮色中湿露的空气，
请记住我
　　犹如信守诺言至死不渝。

A Wish

Joshua Henry Jones, Jr.

When your joys are of the sweetest
And your heart is light and free;
When your griefs are skimming fleetest,
Love, one moment think of me.

I'd not ask you to remember
Me when life is dull and drear;
When your hopes are but an ember
From a cold and vanished year;

Sorrow's far too bleak a burden
To retain in mem'ry's hall.
Friendship has no greater guerdon
Than to happiness recall.

So, when roses scent the twilight
Air with ling'ring dew damp breath,
Please remember me as eye–bright
Faith remembers until death.

夏日暮光

约书亚·亨利·小琼斯

只是一丝淡淡的胭脂
涂抹在金色的天幕；
只是一只鸣鸟的细语
尚未用翅翼包裹它的头；
只是一声轻轻的叹息
当月光明媚的山岭告别微风的时候；
更是森林的挥手告辞
颔首低眉欢快温柔；
只是一缕阳光的亲切致意
祝愿大家安枕无忧；
星星即将重现在黑暗的天际
拉上沾满夜露的暮光帷幕。

In Summer Twilight

Joshua Henry Jones, Jr.

Just a dash of lambent carmine
Shading into sky of gold;
Just a twitter of a song-bird
Ere the wings its head enfold;
Just a rustling sigh of parting
From the moon-kissed hill to breeze;
And a cheerful gentle, nodding
Adieu waving from the trees;
Just a friendly sunbeam's flutter
Wishing all a night's repose,
Ere the stars swing back the curtain
Bringing twilight's dewy close.

新巨人

艾玛·拉撒路①

不同于希腊著名的青铜巨人，
肢体健硕阔步前行；
在我们海洗日浴的大门，这里将矗立
一名高大的妇女手擎火炬，它的火焰
是囚禁的闪电，她的名字
是流亡者的母亲。她手中的灯塔
欢迎来自世界各地的移民；她的温柔眼睛
统率架接雄伟双城的港口海滨。
“古老的大地，留下你的辉煌传奇吧！”她用无声的嘴唇
呐喊。“给我，你精疲力竭的人们，穷困潦倒的人们，
饥寒交迫渴望自由的人们，
被你的富饶海岸无情拒绝的人们。
将这些饱经风霜无家可归的难民送给我，
我在金色大门旁高举明灯！”

① 1849～1887，诗人、翻译家和争取犹太人权益社会活动家。生于纽约一个富裕犹太人家庭，从小接受良好的私塾教育，学习英美文学及德语、法语和意大利语。11岁开始写作，其十四行诗《新巨人》被刻印在自由女神像基座上。

The New Colossus

Emma Lazarus

Not like the brazen giant of Greek fame,
With conquering limbs astride from land to land;
Here at our sea–washed, sunset gates shall stand
A mighty woman with a torch, whose flame
Is the imprisoned lightning, and her name
Mother of Exiles. From her beacon–hand
Glows world–wide welcome; her mild eyes command
The air–bridged harbor that twin cities frame.
"Keep, ancient lands, your storied pomp!" cries she
With silent lips. "Give me your tired, your poor,
Your huddled masses yearning to breathe free,
The wretched refuse of your teeming shore.
Send these, the homeless, tempest–tost to me,
I lift my lamp beside the golden door!"

中秋月

亨利·沃兹沃斯·朗费罗[①]

中秋的月亮！它的神秘光芒
映照在村庄的屋顶和镀金的风标上，
森林的树冠和被遗弃的空巢鸟房
乡村小道上
儿童卧室的落地窗
以及丰收田野和辉煌。
夏天曾来做客的鸟儿已经飞向南方，
辛勤的马车从田间运回最后的草粮。
万物皆是符号征象：
大自然的外观并非变化无常，
犹如鲜花，果实和落叶一样；
那歌声动人的鸟儿随着夏天离去，
仅留下空巢，
和禾草中鹌鹑的鸣唱。

① 1807 ~ 1882，第一位将但丁的《神曲》译成英文的美国作家。生于缅因州波特兰市一个律师家庭，精通拉丁文和意、德、法及西班牙和瑞典等多国语言，曾任哈佛大学当代语言学教授。其诗作风格多样，具有悠扬音乐旋律的美感。

The Harvest Moon

Henry Wadsworth Longfellow

It is the Harvest Moon! On gilded vanes
And roofs of villages, on woodland crests
And their aerial neighborhoods of nests
Deserted, on the curtained window–panes
Of rooms where children sleep, on country lanes
And harvest–fields, its mystic splendor rests!
Gone are the birds that were our summer guests,
With the last sheaves return the laboring wains!
All things are symbols: the external shows
Of Nature have their image in the mind,
As flowers and fruits and falling of the leaves;
The song–birds leave us at the summer's close,
Only the empty nests are left behind,
And pipings of the quail among the sheaves.

秋天

埃米·洛艾尔[①]

他们带给我一枝针叶黄色大丽花，
富贵，奢华。
花朵圆满，
浅绿的花茎笔直挺拔。
金黄的花瓣成熟典雅，
褶边精致耀眼，
一个火球砰然迸发：
旺盛的生育力金光灿烂
昭示天下。
他们带给我一枝针叶黄色大丽花，
可是我已不能接种发芽。
我将花送给你吧？
因为你夺走了
我曾经拥有的青春年华。

① 1874～1925，最早采用自由诗体的美国作家之一，生于波士顿一望族，从小厌学，中学毕业后云游四方，结交社会名流。28岁开始写诗。

Autumn

Amy Lowell

They brought me a quilled, yellow dahlia, Opulent, flaunting.
Round gold
Flung out of a pale green stalk.
Round, ripe gold
Of maturity,
Meticulously frilled and flaming,
A fire–ball of proclamation:
Fecundity decked in staring yellow
For all the world to see.
They brought a quilled, yellow dahlia,
To me who am barren
Shall I send it to you,
You who have taken with you
All I once possessed?

十 年

埃米·洛艾尔

刚来的时候，你犹如红酒和蜂蜜，
味道甜美令我痴迷。
如今你像早晨刚出炉的面包，
圆润适宜。
因为熟知其味我不再细细品尝，
但是我依然获取了所有营养。

A Decade

Amy Lowell

When you came, you were like red wine and honey,
And the taste of you burnt my mouth with its sweetness.
Now you are like morning bread,
Smooth and pleasant.
I hardly taste you at all for I know your savour,
But I am completely nourished.

情歌

米娜·洛伊[1]

我们可能已经楚雨巫云
在独享卧床的时辰
或者倒凤颠鸾
在世俗的圣餐桌上
红酒溅满了淫乱的嘴唇

我们也许生了一只蝴蝶
羽翼上
印着血色的每日新闻

Love Songs

Mina Loy

We might have coupled
In the bed-ridden monopoly of a moment
Or broken flesh with one another
At the profane communion table
Where wine is spilled on promiscuous lips

We might have given birth to a butterfly
With the daily news
Printed in blood on its wings

---

① 1882 ~ 1966，超现实意象派画家和女权主义者。生于英国伦敦，曾就读慕尼黑和巴黎的美术学校，成年后移民美国，在纽约从事艺术创作。其诗歌风格独树一帜，其中有关性的大胆描写被她的同行视为惊世骇俗。

致乔安尼斯

米娜·洛伊

我的双脚
踢着石板栈道
你走过之后留下的痕迹
风将白色街道上的污垢充填到
我的肺和鼻腔
兴奋的小鸟
延续飞行到黑夜
无法抵达目标

To Joannes

Mina Loy

My pair of feet
Smack the flag-stones
That are something left over from your walking
The wind stuffs the scum of the white street
Into my lungs and my nostrils
Exhilarated birds
Prolonging flight into the night
Never reaching — — — — — — —

爱是火焰

乔治·马里恩·麦克凯伦[①]

爱是燃烧的火焰圣光，
令人充满甜蜜的渴望；
然而，一旦圣坛感受到炽热的呼吸，
心便成为锻造的熔炉直到死亡。

爱是生命琼浆，
爱是欣喜若狂；
你可以用任何辞藻来形容爱，
但是心知道，爱意味痛苦悲伤。

Love Is a Flame

George Marion McClellan

Love is a flame that burns with sacred fire,
And fills the being up with sweet desire;
Yet, once the altar feels love's fiery breath,
The heart must be a crucible till death.

Say love is life; and say it not amiss,
That love is but a synonym for bliss.
Say what you will of love—in what refrain,
But knows the heart, 'tis but a word for pain.

① 1860 ~ 1934，非裔诗人和神父，生于田纳西州。大学毕业后，曾多年在黑人学校担任拉丁文和英文教师，并出版了两部以宗教、大自然和爱情为主题的诗集。

日落密西西比

乔治·马里恩·麦克凯伦

日落西沉多么美丽，
　　余晖映照在密西西比。
我站在河岸
　　看见河水奔流不息，
涌动的河水
　　犹如躁动不安的灵魂，
汹涌澎湃地追逐
　　渐行渐远的目的地。

日落西沉多么美丽，
　　滚滚潮流奔腾不息。
已故亲人的阴魂
　　在浪波上舞动消失；
在亲人的短暂幻影中，
　　他们的脸上洋溢着欢喜，
在水雾中招手致意，
　　然后向大海奔去。

日落西沉多么美丽，
　　我独立河边默默沉思。
凝视奔流的河水，
　　聆听它的不安与叹息；
曾经的渴望和梦想，
　　已经变得模糊而遥不可及，
就像无尽的河水，
　　从我的心中涌动流逝。

日落西沉多么美丽，
　　太阳静静地入眠休息，
留下金色的余晖
　　映照在巨大的密西西比胸膛里；
在暮色即将降临的河面上
　　反射跳跃折光熠熠，
好似亲吻河水晚安，
　　抚慰躁动汹涌的潮汐。

The Sun Went Down In Beauty

George Marion McClellan

The sun went down in beauty
　　Beyond the Mississippi side,
As I stood on the banks of the river
　　And watched its waters glide;
Its swelling currents resembling
　　The longing restless soul,
Surging, swelling, and pursuing
　　Its ever receding goal.

The sun went down in beauty,
　　But the restless tide flowed on,
And the phantom of absent loved ones
　　Danced on the waves and were gone;
Fleeting phantoms of loved ones,
　　Their faces jubilant with glee,
In the spray seemed to rise and beckon,
　　And then rush on to the sea.

The sun went down in beauty,
While I stood musing alone,
Stood watching the rushing river
And heard its restless moan;
Longings, vague, intenable,
So far from speech apart,
Like the endless rush of the river,
Went surging through my heart.

The sun went down in beauty,
Peacefully sank to rest,
Leaving its golden reflection
On the great Mississippi's breast;
Gleaming on the turbulent river,
In the coming gray twilight,
Soothing its restless surging,
And kissing its waters goodnight.

冬月蒲公英

乔治·马里恩·麦克凯伦

纳什维尔是如此寒冷！四处
盖满从荒漠吹来的沙尘，
透过冬月的天空，
只见雪花飘落纷纷。
哦，单纯的蒲公英！你被几个
暖日误导从冬眠中苏醒，
愚蠢地提前开花报春。
但是，你已灿烂辉煌，黄色的精灵！
尽管如今你被冻结在瘦弱的花茎
很多人都怀有对你的感恩。
爱的炽热和心颤渐渐离去，
寒冷的大雪慢慢降临，
心也许仍会跳动，但是绽放和凋亡
将光顾所有旺盛的生命。

A January Dandelion

George Marion McClellan

All Nashville is a–chill! And everywhere,
As wind–swept sands upon the deserts blow,
There is, each moment, sifted through the air,
A powered blast of January snow.
O thoughtless Dandelion! to be misled
By a few warm days to leave thy natural bed,
Was folly growth and blooming over soon.
And yet, thou blasted, yellow–coated gem!
Full many hearts have but a common boon
With thee, now freezing on thy slender stem.
When once the heart–blooms by love’s fervid breath
Is left, and chilling snow is sifted in,
It still may beat, but there is blast and death
To all that blooming life that might have been.

玫瑰之心

乔治·马里恩·麦克凯伦

我将我的灵魂和博大的爱
　　藏在这朵玫瑰的心房，
它的呼吸将带着我的爱
　　弥漫四方。

也许她会采摘这朵玫瑰，
　　随着羞涩的红晕掠过她的脸庞，
将我隐藏的秘密
　　吸进她纯洁的心脏。

我将生活在她的怀抱
　　和甜蜜的气场，
沉迷于一阵狂喜，
　　胜过极乐天堂。

In the Heart of a Rose

George Marion McClellan

I will hide my soul and its mighty love
In the bosom of this rose,
And its dispensing breath will take
My love wherever it goes.

And perhaps she'll pluck this very rose,
And, quick as blushes start,
Will breathe my hidden secret in
Her unsuspecting heart.

And there I will live in her embrace
And the realm of sweetness there,
Enamored with an ecstasy,
Of bliss beyond compare.

另类

克洛德·麦凯[①]

虽被身体束缚，我的精神渴望
那个我的父辈曾经生活过的灰暗地方。
略有感受但从未所闻的言语，我的嘴唇会讲；
久被遗忘的丛林歌曲，我的灵魂会唱。
我愿回到那个平和的黑色世界，
但是强大的西方将我捆绑。
当屈膝向陌生的神灵祈祷时，
我永远不能奢望被完全释放。
我失去了某些至关重要的东西，
内心无限迷惘。
形同幽灵走在人生道路上，
在熙攘的人群中孤独彷徨。
因为我出生异域远离故乡，
在白人的威胁下，黯然神伤。

① 1889 ~ 1948，知名的非裔诗人、作家和哈莱姆黑人文艺复兴运动中心人物。生于牙买加，13岁赴美求学，毕业于堪萨斯州立大学。其诗歌充满了对种族歧视和社会偏见的愤恨。

Outcast

Claude McKay

For the dim regions whence my fathers came
My spirit, bondaged by the body, longs.
Words felt, but never heard, my lips would frame;
My soul would sing forgotten jungle songs.
I would go back to darkness and to peace,
But the great western world holds me in fee,
And I may never hope for full release
While to its alien gods I bend my knee.
Something in me is lost, forever lost,
Some vital thing has gone out of my heart,
And I must walk the way of life a ghost
Among the sons of earth, a thing apart;
For I was born, far from my native clime,
Under the white man's menace, out of time.

致冬季

克洛德·麦凯

留步，静爱和灵雪之季!
阳光里带有一丝微妙的甜蜜，
溪流中泛着阵阵欢乐的涟漪，
白昼的长度与日俱增，
迎面而來的风格外喧闹充满活力。
鸟儿的歌声更加欢愉，
顽皮嬉戏的松鼠
从枫树之冠扔下枯黄的细枝。
我阅读这些含蓄的征兆，理解它们的旨意:
我知道你准备离去。
哦，请留步!我逃离的故土四季葱绿，
还有轻轻摇曳的棕榈，
微风和煦，蓝色溪流波光熠熠，
给我悲痛的心温暖慰藉。

To Winter

Claude McKay

Stay, season of calm love and soulful snows!
There is a subtle sweetness in the sun,
The ripples on the stream's breast gaily run,
The wind more boisterously by me blows,
And each succeeding day now longer grows.
The birds a gladder music have begun,
The squirrel, full of mischief and of fun,
From maple's topmost branch the brown twig throws.
I read these pregnant signs, know what they mean:
I know that thou art making ready to go.
Oh stay! I fled a land where fields are green
Always, and palms wave gently to and fro,
And winds are balmy, blue brooks ever sheen,
To ease my heart of its impassioned woe.

躺平

克洛德·麦凯

奴性的恐惧没有削弱我的意志
　　今天早晨，我鼓起勇气对自己说
我将懒惰，坚定不移，
　　我今天不会浪费时间辛苦劳作。

行尸走肉的喧嚣世界，
　　将不会打扰我安息中的平静梦想，
四堵墙壁使我免受狂叫着的食尸鬼的伤害，
　　尘世所有的仇恨都逃离了我安宁的胸膛。

我将懒洋洋地躺卧在此，完全清醒，
　　我心安理得地躺下只为做梦，
忘却世上的辛劳和爱情
　　没有半点思考或活动的冲动。

我是多么疲惫，简直累得快死！
　　今天我放下所有负担，
就像草地上的一个孩子
　　在南方的阳光下，我躺下偷懒。

我感到环抱身体的床舒适温馨，
　　力量在我的骨髓中轻轻流淌，
我忧虑重重的大脑漫游进入梦境，
　　生活犹如动听的歌曲柔美悠扬。

French Leave

Claude McKay

No servile little fear shall daunt my will
    This morning, I have courage steeled to say
I will be lazy, conqueringly still,
    I will not lose the hours in toil this day.

The roaring world without, careless of souls,
    Shall leave me to my placid dream of rest,
My four walls shield me from its shouting ghouls,
    And all its hates have fled my quiet breast.

And I will loll here resting, wide awake,
    Dead to the world of work, the world of love,
I laze contented just for dreaming's sake,
    With not the slightest urge to think or move.

How tired unto death, how tired I was!
    Now for a day I put my burdens by,
And like a child amidst the meadow grass
    Under the southern sun, I languid lie,

And feel the bed about me kindly deep,
    My strength ooze gently from my hollow bones,
My worried brain drift aimlessly to sleep,
    Life soften to a song of tuneful tones.

母亲的勇气

埃德娜·文森特·米蕾[①]

母亲的勇气随她离去，
依然与她在一起：
犹如一块从新英格兰开采的岩石；
如今回归花岗岩的山脊。

母亲的黄金胸针首饰
留给我佩戴珍惜；
没有什么比它更宝贵：
但是它并非我必有的东西。

哦，假如她留给我
她带进坟墓的东西！——
那岩石般的勇气和胆识，
对她已毫无意义，而正是我之所需。

① 1892～1950，极富声誉的诗人，剧作家和倡导妇女权利的社会活动家。生于缅因州一个贫困家庭，从中学开始便显露出超常的诗歌天赋，其作品在报刊上发表，获得包括普利策在内多项大奖。从瓦萨尔学院毕业后到纽约曼哈顿从事文学创作。

The Courage That My Mother Had

Edna St. Vincent Millay

The courage that my mother had
Went with her, and is with her still:
Rock from New England quarried;
Now granite in a granite hill.

The golden brooch my mother wore
She left behind for me to wear;
I have no thing I treasure more:
Yet, it is something I could spare.

Oh, if instead she'd left to me
The thing she took into the grave!—
That courage like a rock, which she
Has no more need of, and I have.

纪 念

埃德娜·文森特·米蕾

仅仅一两个雨天
在那个风疾的塔楼上，
那便是我所拥有你的一切——
大约三十分钟时间。

过往行人故弄玄虚的寒暄
在那条煤渣铺就的小径，
赤条条的黑莓丛边
天色渐暗 紫霭幽潜。

我仍记得
你的片语碎言，
和你穿的那件丑陋外套，
黑白格子镶嵌。

仅仅一两个雨天
和一句苦涩的再见。
为什么你仍像一只云雀
让我怀念？

Souvenir

Edna St. Vincent Millay

Just a rainy day or two
In a windy tower,
That was all I had of you—
Saving half an hour.

Marred by greeting passing groups
In a cinder walk,
Near some naked blackberry hoops
Dim with purple chalk.

I remember three or four
Things you said in spite,
And an ugly coat you wore,
Plaided black and white.

Just a rainy day or two
And a bitter word.
Why do I remember you
As a singing bird?

夏季之爱（十四行诗第二十七）

埃德娜·文森特·米蕾

我知道，在你的心里我只是夏日，
而非一年之中完整的四季；
你必须从它处获得如此高贵的品质，
因为它们不属于我，亲爱的。
我没有可供出售的金黄果实，
也没有任何智慧和冰冷的东西；
我已深沉地爱你如此之久，
不可能依然保持春天的甜蜜。
因此我说：亲爱的，夏天离去，
我也必须踏着无声的鼓点悄然消失。
我伴随夏天回到你身边，
你可以重新欢呼玫瑰和鸟儿。
否则的话，过不了多久，
你将另寻红颜知己。

I know I am but summer to your heart

(Sonnet XXVII)

Edna St. Vincent Millay

I know I am but summer to your heart,
And not the full four seasons of the year;
And you must welcome from another part
Such noble moods as are not mine, my dear.
No gracious weight of golden fruits to sell
Have I, nor any wise and wintry thing;
And I have loved you all too long and well
To carry still the high sweet breast of Spring.
Wherefore I say: O love, as summer goes,
I must be gone, steal forth with silent drums,
That you may hail anew the bird and rose
When I come back to you, as summer comes.
Else will you seek, at some not distant time,
Even your summer in another clime.

潮 石

埃德娜·文森特·米蕾

这些被潮汐浸润过的岩石，
　　带着白色的甲壳虫和褐色的海草
纤细的底部呈现美丽的青绿，
　　这些岩石在潮汐退去时突兀孤傲
涨潮时又将
　　变得昏暗危险，遥不可及
不是梦想而是死亡的地方——
　　回归阴森的海底。
有一个小孩在巨人的房子里
终日游荡——
房子里充满了新奇，
　　但不是一个适合孩子玩耍的游乐场。

Low-Tide

Edna St. Vincent Millay

These wet rocks where the tide has been,
　　Barnacled white and weeded brown
And slimed beneath to a beautiful green,
　　These wet rocks where the tide went down
Will show again when the tide is high
　　Faint and perilous, far from shore,
No place to dream, but a place to die,—
　　The bottom of the sea once more.
There was a child that wandered through
　　A giant's empty house all day,—
House full of wonderful things and new,
　　But no fit place for a child to play.

冬晨

威廉·H.A. 摩尔[1]

此时正是冬天的早晨，爱神，
我看见阳光下变色的树叶
对着蔚蓝的天空燃烧得明亮热烈，
此时正是冬天的早晨，爱神，
此时正是冬天的早晨，爱神，
我听到低沉变调的钟声
终日在空中清脆奏鸣，
此时正是冬天的早晨，爱神，
我听到钟声，我看见变化的叶子，
一颗孤单的心为夏天默默悲戚，
此时正是冬天的早晨，爱神。

Here in the Time of the Winter Morn

William H. A. Moore

Here in the time of the Winter morn, Love,
I see the Sunlit leaves of changing hue
Burn clear against a sky of tender blue,
Here in the time of the Winter morn, Love.
Here in the time of the Winter morn, Love,
I hear the low tone bells of changing song
Ring clear upon the air the full day long,
Here in the time of the Winter morn, Love.
I hear the bells, I see the changing leaves,
And one lone heart for Summer silent grieves,
Here in the time of the Winter morn, Love.

① 生卒年月不详，非裔诗人和新闻工作者。生于纽约市，曾就读纽约城市大学，并在哥伦比亚大学学习。1922 年其诗集《暮歌》（*Dusk Song*）出版。

反复

多萝西·帕克[①]

我们的良辰将会到来。
请牵着我的手静静地走
在小路上徘徊，
在山岭中漫游。

重新相爱多么快乐；
仰望焕然一新的蓝天，
拾起闲置已久的笔墨，
甜蜜地书写苍白的谎言。

描绘破碎滴血的心，
述说绵延不绝的情，
对天发誓，然后却各奔前程，
时好时坏，时合时分。

这个美丽的故事结局如何
我们不必事先知道；
我们中的一个爱得越多，
那么另外一个爱得越少。

---

① 1893～1967，讽刺作家、评论家、剧作家及诗人。生于新泽西州，在纽约曼哈顿长大。母亲是苏格兰人后裔，父亲是犹太商人。4岁时母亲因病去世，不久父亲再婚。她与继母关系紧张，并受父亲虐待。18岁便开始发表诗歌，先后在《名利场》和*Vogue*时尚杂志工作，是《纽约客》杂志创刊编辑之一。共发表了300多首诗歌。其作品短小精悍，诙谐幽默，常以她个人荒诞不经的风流韵事为题材。

如此这般，周而复始；
亲爱的，我们将有属于自己的那一天。
玫瑰无可奈何死去
新的蓓蕾将在来年再现。

Recurrence

Dorothy Parker

We shall have our little day.
Take my hand and travel still
Round and round the little way,
Up and down the little hill.

It is good to love again;
Scan the renovated skies,
Dip and drive the idling pen,
Sweetly tint the paling lies.

Trace the dripping, pierc è d heart,
Speak the fair, insistent verse,
Vow to God, and slip apart,
Little better, little worse.

Would we need not know before
How shall end this prettiness;
One of us must love the more,
One of us shall love the less.

Thus it is, and so it goes;
We shall have our day, my dear.
Where, unwilling, dies the rose
Buds the new, another year.

勿忘我

安·柏拉图[①]

晨雾迷离，
阳光轻抚鲜花草地；
你面带友善的微笑，
而且坚信心心相依，
你寻求永恒的安息，
　　请不要将我忘记。

最后一缕暮光降临，
你在殿堂踱步不止；
夜雾在山上聚集，
周围一切变得静寂，
唯有山间小溪的绵言细语，
　　请不要将我忘记。

第一颗灿烂的星星，
孤独地照射在黑暗的天际；
明月驱散忧郁，
繁星闪烁，
犹如中午的太阳光彩熠熠，
　　请不要将我忘记。

风中飘着沉重的叹息，
你陷入深思极虑；

---

① 1824～？，美国历史上第一位出版诗集的黑人妇女。生长于康涅狄格州，有黑人和印地安人血统，她是一所黑人学校的教师。

如果你因为孤独
而哀声叹气，
或者愁苦忧郁，
请不要将我忘记。

鸟儿不再久久等待你，
连它的晨歌也无心顾及；
你搜寻不朽的典籍，
或者倾听一个古老的先智，
用他的灵魂遏制你的悲愤，
请不要将我忘记。

你默默无语，
自我封闭；
你在无尽的深渊，
沉睡安息；
如果我们在人间不能再见，
请不要将我忘记。

你的容光将长留于世，
你会铭记亲人的悲泣；
在遗忘的阴影下，
毫无生息的棺木被安葬于地，
装着你的尘世身躯，
请不要将我忘记。

“如果悲伤充塞你未来的日子，
终日掩面而泣，
记住，尽管我们注定要分离，
但有一颗怡悦而诚实的心，
永远不会忘记你。”

Forget Me Not

Ann Plato

When in the morning's misty hour,
When the sun beams gently o'er each flower;
When thou dost cease to smile benign,
And think each heart responds with thine,
When seeking rest among divine,
Forget me not.

When the last rays of twilight fall,
And thou art pacing yonder hall;
When mists are gathering on the hill,
Nor sound is heard save mountain rill,
When all around bids peace be still,
Forget me not.

When the first star with brilliance bright,
Gleams lonely o'er the arch of night;
When the bright moon dispels the gloom,
And various are the stars that bloom,
And brighten as the sun at noon,
Forget me not.

When solemn sighs the hollow wind,
And deepen'd thought enraps the mind;
If e'er thou doest in mournful tone,
E'er sigh because thou feel alone,
Or wrapt in melancholy prone,
Forget me not.

When bird does wait thy absence long,
Nor tend unto its morning song;
While thou art searching stoic page,
Or listening to an ancient sage,
Whose spirit curbs a mournful rage,
        Forget me not.

Then when in silence thou doest walk,
Nor being round with whom to talk;
When thou art on the mighty deep,
And do in quiet action sleep;
If we no more on earth do meet,
        Forget me not.

When brightness round thee long shall bloom,
And knelt remembering those in gloom;
And when in deep oblivion's shade,
This breathless, mouldering form is laid,
And thy terrestrial body staid,
        Forget me not.

"Should sorrow cloud thy coming years,
And bathe thy happiness in tears,
Remember, though we're doom'd to part,
There lives one fond and faithful heart,
        That will forget thee not."

隐居

亚历山大·波西[1]

松林履盖的崇山峻岭
　　横亘在我与喧嚣之间；
尘土飞扬的生活之路
　　无法抵达我隐居的林泉。

我听到晨风苏醒，
　　轻拂紫色的山巅，
以及晨曦中
　　湖面上的睡莲。

回声和歌神与我同住，
　　美神邀我相见，
我们欢聚在
　　她的壮丽宫殿。

群山将我紧紧包围，
　　仅留头上一片蓝天。
风景四季优美，
　　空气日夜甘甜。

---

① 1873 ~ 1908，诗人和幽默作家。生于俄克拉何马州一个印地安人保护区，父亲是苏格兰人，母亲是塔斯基吉部落后裔。1901 年创办了第一份印地安人日报。其诗歌以描绘印地安人生活环境的自然风光为主。35 岁时试图通过洪水泛滥的河流时不幸遇难。

我听见河水细语轻言
　　问候沿岸的沙滩草甸；
凝望午夜的天空
　　银河繁星点点。

万籁俱寂，
　　夜色深潜，
且听轻风漫步于山林，
　　美妙如仙。

雪松为我搭起帐篷，
　　我在林海中睡眠。
在那神奇的房间，
　　我的自由广阔无边！

梦幻般的的南风温柔拂面，
　　像一只饱食花粉的蜜蜂缄默无言。
轻风在林中叹息，
　　伴随悠扬的音律和弦。

落日余辉耀眼，
　　暮色徐徐蔓延。
哦，待到玫瑰色的曙光初现，
　　群山欢唱 歌声满天。

在孤寂的高空，
　　苍鹰久久盘旋，
犹如飞翔的精灵，
　　直到它的身影渐行渐远。

My Hermitage

Alexander Posey

Between me and the noise of strife
　　Are walls of mountains set with pine;
The dusty, care–strewn paths of life
　　Lead not to this retreat of mine.

I hear the morning wind awake
　　Beyond the purple height,
And, in the growing light,
　　The lap of lilies on the lake.

I live with Echo and with Song,
　　And Beauty leads me forth to see
Her temple's colonnades, and long
　　Together do we love to be.

The mountains wall me in, complete,
　　And leave me but a bit blue
Above.　　All year, the days are sweet—
　　How sweet! And all the long nights thro'

I hear the river flowing by
　　Along its sandy bars;
Behold, far in the midnight sky,
　　An infinite of stars!

'Tis sweet, when all is still,
　　When darkness gathers round,
To hear, from hill to hill,
　　The far, the wandering sound.

The cedar and the pine
        Have pitched their tents with me.
What freedom vast is mine!
        What room! What mystery!

Upon the dreamy southern breeze,
        That steals in like a laden bee
And sighs for rest among the trees,
        Are far–blown bits of melody.

What afterglows the twilight hold,
        The darkening skies along!
And O, what rose–like dawns unfold,
        That smite the hills to song!

High in the solitude of air,
        The gray hawk circles on and on,
Till, like a spirit soaring there,
        His image pales and he is gone!

山岭黎明

亚历山大·波西

看哪，我用牵牛花天蓝色的花朵当作杯具
畅饮花蜜
早晨溅洒的银露；
以及轻风的音律
在林间枝头
追逐嬉戏。

看哪，我有无数稀贵的珍珠钻石
我呼吸黄金般的空气
我的房间光芒四射；
我的生活犹如梦幻一样神奇
在我的山中小屋
当黎明破晓之时。

On the Hills of Dawn

Alexander Posey

Behold, the morning–glory's sky–blue cup
Is mine wherewith to drink the nectar up
That morning spills of silver dew,
And song upon the winds that woo
And sigh their vows
Among the boughs!

Behold, I'm rich in diamonds rare,
And pearls, and breathe a golden air;
My room is filled with shattered beams
Of light; my life is one of dreams,
In my hut on
The hills of dawn.

海 贝

亚历山大·波西

我拾起带着宝石红嘴唇的贝壳
　　它们轻声叙说海里的生活，
曾几何时，我凝视海上的帆船
　　乘着白色的翅膀，飞驶而过。

那天所见的远航帆船
　　在我的记忆里已经变得隐隐约约；
但是我依然听到，从遥远的地方，
　　蓝色的海浪不停地追逐唱歌。

Seashells

Alexander Posey

I picked up shells with ruby lips
　　That spoke in whispers of the sea,
Upon a time, and watched the ships,
　　On white wings, sail away to sea.

The ships I saw go out that day
　　Live misty—dim in memory;
But still I hear, from far away,
　　The blue waves breaking ceaselessly.

秋 天

亚历山大·波西

午后的寂静
犹如梦境，
一块金色的天幕
在森林草原的上空织成；
刚刚从天而降的松鸭
絮叨不停，
热情的问候娓娓动听，
漫天的红叶
在空中飞舞，
一如既往绚丽缤纷，
随着一声无谓的叹息
秋天已经来临。

Autumn

Alexander Posey

In the dreamy silence
Of the afternoon, a
Cloth of gold is woven
Over wood and prairie;
And the jaybird, newly
Fallen from the heaven,
Scatters cordial greetings,
And the air is filled with
Scarlet leaves, that, dropping,
Rise again, as ever,
With a useless sigh for
Rest—and it is Autumn.

七 月

亨丽埃塔·科迪利亚·雷①

天空骄阳艳丽，
光影在林中嘻戏，
中午的田野色彩斑澜
　　疲倦的牛羊正在那里恬息。
溪水从葱郁的山间缓缓流下，
音乐多么甜蜜！
金星闪亮升起
遐想悠然而去。

July

Henrietta Cordelia Ray

Sunshine and shadow play amid the trees
In bosky groves, while from the vivid sky
The sun's gold arrows fleck the fields at noon,
　　Where weary cattle to their slumber hie.
How sweet the music of the purling rill,
Trickling adown the grassy hill!
While dreamy fancies come to give repose
When the first star of evening glows.

---

① 1849 ~ 1917，非裔教师和诗人。生于纽约市一个牧师家庭，毕业于纽约城市大学。其赞美诗《林肯》在 1876 年 4 月举行的废除奴隶制纪念碑揭幕典礼上宣读。诗集《十四行诗》1893 年出版，具有重要的文学和社会价值。

过往

凯尔·杨·赖斯[①]

一片黑色的帆影，
犹如野鹅的翅羽，
隐现于落日黄昏。
月亮即将带来耀眼的白银
照明夜空
以及那些永生的
远行移民
万世不朽的星星。

Passage

Cale Young Rice

A dark sail,
Like a wild-goose wing,
Where the sunset was.
The moon soon will silver its sinewy flight
Thro the night watches,
And the far flight
Of those immortal migrants,
The ever-returning stars.

① 1872 ~ 1943，诗人和剧作家。生于肯塔基州一个烟草商人家庭，毕业于哈佛大学。

十月的山岭

约翰·罗林·瑞杰[1]

我望着紫色的山岭
　　由近及远逶迤上升，
它们的沉静触动我的灵魂
　　它们的美丽慰藉我的心。

生活的烦恼艰辛，
　　了无踪影。
清静的群山中，
　　哪有劳苦与纷争？

胸中的痛苦埋藏至深，
　　只有山峦叠嶂能够触及减轻。
虽然我们无言以对，
　　群山代表安息永恒。

神秘的群山魅力迷人——
　　给我抚慰和温馨。
每当陷入悲伤的情绪中，
　　我便投身于群山之中的寂静。

群山是如此平静坚忍，
　　对自己的分量充满自信！
我们与它们一起挺立，
　　脚踏残酷的时代命运。

---

① 1827 ~ 1867，美国最早的印地安人小说家。生于佐治亚州一个印地安人部落，父亲是切诺基部落首领，母亲是白人。

从深不可测的地层，
　　山灵直冲浮云。
犹如一座恬静飞升的金字塔，
　　带着我们与天使同行。

我不会忘却这个安息的意境，
　　以及梦幻般的快乐欢欣；
它已烙印在我的灵魂，
　　铭刻于我的内心。

October Hills

John Rollin Ridge

I look upon the purple hills
　　That rise in steps to yonder peaks,
And all my soul their silence thrills
　　And to my heart their beauty speaks.

What now to me the jars of life,
　　Its petty cares, its harder throes?
The hills are free from toil and strife,
　　And clasp me in their deep repose.

They soothe the pain within my breast
　　No power but theirs could ever reach,
They emblem that eternal rest
　　We cannot compass in our speech.

From far I feel their secret charm—
    From far they shed their healing balm,
And lost to sense of grief or harm
    I plunge within their pulseless calm.

How full of peace and strength they stand,
    Self-poised and conscious of their weight!
We rise with them, that silent band,
    Above the wrecks of Time or Fate;

For, mounting from their depths unseen,
    Their spirit pierces upward, far,
A soaring pyramid serene,
    And lifts us where the angels are.

I would not lose this scene of rest,
    Nor shall its dreamy joy depart;
Upon my soul it is imprest,
    And pictured in my inmost heart.

随想

约翰·罗林·瑞杰

我凝视她的双眼——它们的柔情之光，
坚定不移，将我心灵的至暗之夜照亮，
如同远方璀璨的星星
将银色的光芒抛洒在我的身上。

我的心中燃烧着甜美的幻想，
所见之处皆是天堂；
凭借她深情的目光
万物变得倍加可爱令人神往。

我触碰她温顺的小手——犹如一只平和的鸽子
带着真诚的爱意，停歇在我的手上；
我被一股深邃的力量感动，
心如火焰，血脉膨胀。

我对着鲜花呼出她的名字：鲜花顿放
带着更珍稀的色彩，散发更浓郁的芬芳！
展翅翱翔的云雀听到她的名字，
它的晨歌更加甜美悠扬。

哦，多么神奇的名字！深深地铭刻在我的心上，
那个名字属于她，我也像那个名字一样！
那个名字令我日日冥思，
夜夜默想！

Random Thoughts of Her

John Rollin Ridge

I gaze into her eyes—their tender light,
And strong, illumes my spirit's darkest night,
And pours rich glory on me as a star
Which brings its silver luster from afar.

Sweet thoughts and beautiful within me burn,
And heaven I see what way soe'er I turn;
In borrowed radiance of her soulful glance
All things grow tenfold lovely and entrance.

I touch her willing hand—as gentle dove
It rests within my own, in trusting love;
And yet it moves me with a power so deep,
My heart is flame, and all my pulses leap.

I breathe her name unto the flowers: they bloom
With rarer hues, and shed more rich perfume!
The skylark hears it, as he floats along,
And adds new sweetness to his morning song.

Oh magic name! deep graven on my heart,
And, as its owner, of myself a part!
It hath in all my daily thoughts a share,
And forms the burden of my nightly prayer!

母亲

萝拉·瑞杰[1]

您的爱犹如月光一样
将丑陋的事物变成美好的景象，
让卑微的灵魂
在朦胧之中相得益彰

就像在破镜里……
因为您的精神光芒
他们的形象，
在闪耀的光束中变得明亮
从而爱戴您点石成金的力量。

您在我的脑海里的形象
更似一缕荧光
我看见您在微弱的光线中
犹如星光照在一堵灰墙上……
就像一只白天鹅的倒影
在水波上忽隐忽现粼粼荡漾。

① 1873 ~ 1941，早期现代派诗人。生于爱尔兰都柏林市，3 岁丧父，幼年随母亲移居新西兰。30 岁时独自带着 3 岁儿子移居澳大利亚，在悉尼艺术学院学习绘画。34 岁移居美国，先后在旧金山和纽约曼哈顿从事绘画和诗歌创作。因生活所迫曾充当艺术模特以及在工厂上班，对贫困工薪阶层充满理解和同情，并积极参与社会抗议活动。其作品充分反映了她的激进政治理念，对美国当代诗歌具有一定影响。

Mother

Lola Ridge

Your love was like moonlight
turning harsh things to beauty,
so that little wry souls
reflecting each other obliquely

as in cracked mirrors...
beheld in your luminous spirit
their own reflection,
transfigured as in a shining stream,
and loved you for what they are not.

You are less an image in my mind
than a luster
I see you in gleams
pale as star–light on a gray wall...
evanescent as the reflection of a white swan
shimmering in broken water.

雨韵

林·里格斯[①]

来自空旷的天边，
绵绵细雨——
给一望无际的农田
带来万分欣喜。

出自黎明的昏茫——
突兀灿烂，
火红的太阳
将寂静的黑暗驱散。

走出生活的阴沉，
走出不可原谅的邪恶，
飘过我贫瘠灰暗的灵魂——
这些歌。

① 1899～1954，杰出剧作家。生于俄克拉何马州一个农场，母亲是切诺基部落后裔。年轻时曾为《洛杉矶时报》《华尔街日报》等多家报刊撰稿，并在俄克拉何马大学教授英文。共发表21部剧本。其中最著名的作品是根据其剧本《丁香绿了》改编的音乐剧《俄克拉荷马！》。

Rhythm of Rain

Lynn Riggs

Out of the barrenness of earth,
And the meager rain—
Mile upon mile of exultant
Fields of grain.

Out of the dimness of morning—
Sudden and stark,
A hot sun dispelling
The hushed dark.

Out of the bleakness of living,
Out of the unforgivable wrongs,
Out of the thin, dun soil of my soul—
These songs.

麦 捆

埃德温·阿灵顿·罗宾逊[①]

风影已在那里涌动很久，
绿麦正在变化成熟；
好像有某种巨大的魔法相助
大地慢慢变成了黄金之洲。
没有任何商品如此平凡朴素
它的躯体和心灵都在那里等候；
带着某种深邃的冥思眼眸
它越沉默越意味深厚。

在这样一片并非公平的土地上，
公平的日子一天接着一天奔流
成千上万金色的麦捆在那里静躺，
它们闪光发亮但不会停留太久——
犹如成千上万的金发女郎
会从她们睡觉的地方起身离走。

① 1869～1935，生长于缅因州，曾就读哈佛大学，因父亲去世家庭困难而辍学。他从小抑郁悲观，中学时便开始用诗歌表达自己的情感。辍学回家务农不久，因失恋迁居纽约专事诗歌创作，并于1896年自费出版了第一部诗集。他本打算用这本诗集给母亲一个惊喜。可母亲在收到诗集前因白喉病故。作者在贫困潦倒中坚持写作。其第二部诗集得到时任总统西奥多·罗斯福青睐。因其作品的独特艺术表现力，他在1920年代三次荣获普利策诗歌奖，并多次进入诺贝尔文学奖候选人名单。

The Sheaves

Edwin Arlington Robinson

Where long the shadows of the wind had rolled,
Green wheat was yielding to the change assigned;
And as by some vast magic undivined
The world was turning slowly into gold.
Like nothing that was ever bought or sold
It waited there, the body and the mind;
And with a mighty meaning of a kind
That tells the more the more it is not told.

So in a land where all days are not fair,
Fair days went on till on another day
A thousand golden sheaves were lying there,
Shining and still, but not for long to stay—
As if a thousand girls with golden hair
Might rise from where they slept and go away.

独白

卡尔·桑德伯格[1]

雨滴的单调独奏优美动听，
那时急时缓
反复无常的天籁之音。

山顶的日出壮美绝伦，
或海上落日西沉，
晚霞流火溢金。

我熟悉的面容美丽动人——
带着天空和大海的多彩神韵，
与和风细雨的安祥恬静。

① 1878 ~ 1967，诗人、传记作家和编辑。生于伊利诺伊州一个瑞典移民家庭，13岁辍学，当过马车夫，泥瓦工，在部队服役五年。退伍后任多家报社记者。其诗作广受读者喜爱，诗集两获普利策奖，对美国当代文学有重要影响。

Monotone

Carl Sandburg

The monotone of the rain is beautiful,
And the sudden rise and slow relapse
Of the long multitudinous rain.

The sun on the hills is beautiful,
Or a captured sunset sea-flung,
Bannered with fire and gold.

A face I know is beautiful—
With fire and gold of sky and sea,
And the peace of long warm rain.

祷告（致外公 惊闻他的奇佩瓦血统被歪曲）

简·约翰斯顿·斯库克拉夫特[①]

起来，最勇敢的酋长！高贵野鹿的象征
　　带着雄鹰的眼光
　　展现您的长矛锋芒，
重新挥舞您的战矛标枪！
　　您的敌人，
　　生性胆小轻狂，
竟敢用黑色的嫉妒抹灭事实，
造谣惑众污蔑您年轻时的英雄形象。

他们说您是一个从苏族虏夺来的孩子，
　　而且徒劳无为地，
　　贬低您的名望
将您的勇士血统视作残暴鲁莽；
　　因为他们知道我们的部落
　　来自遥远的地方，
您作为我们尊贵的首领早已死亡，
您的弓箭已经松弛，您的高傲灵魂不知去向。

您的英雄事迹怎能被遗忘？
　　即使如今的凡人
　　仍然怀想，

---

① 1800 ~ 1842，最早的印地安人作家之一。生长在密歇根北部大湖地区一个印地安人部落，母亲是奇佩瓦酋长女儿，父亲是苏格兰人。她是历史上第一个使用奥吉布瓦语写诗并将奥吉布瓦歌谣翻译成英文的作家，在北美印第安人文学发展进程中占有特殊地位。

您立马横刀的形象，
　　那些曾与您并肩战斗的勇士
　　铭记您的高傲阳刚。
您带着勇气和愤怒奔赴疆场，
部落的敌人闻风丧胆溃败逃亡。

勇士怎能忘记您的崇高辉煌？
　　就像西天的星星一样
　　日落夜降，
您的光芒令敌人神色惊慌。
　　流言蜚语
　　造谣中伤
何以击退您的振臂呐喊？
您的英雄壮举必将驳斥污蔑诽谤。

安息吧，最崇高的酋长！安息于黑暗的土房。
　　您的壮举和名字
　　将万古流芳，
在黑森林与大地之间回响。
　　虽然您的灵魂已经回归
　　到逝者的山上，
然而您的名字将铭刻在我的心房，
被永远珍惜直到勇气和爱消亡。

Invocation

(To my Maternal Grand–father on hearing his descent from Chippewa ancestors misrepresented)

Jane Johnston Schoolcraft

Rise bravest chief! of the mark of the noble deer,
With eagle glance,
Resume thy lance,
And wield again thy warlike spear!
The foes of thy line,
With coward design,
Have dared with black envy to garble the truth,
And stain with a falsehood thy valorous youth.

They say when a child, thou wert ta'en from the Sioux,
And with impotent aim,
To lessen thy fame
Thy warlike lineage basely abuse;
For they know that our band,
Tread a far distant land,
And thou noble chieftain art nerveless and dead,
Thy bow all unstrung, and thy proud spirit fled.

Can the sports of thy youth, or thy deeds ever fade?
Or those e'er forget,
Who are mortal men yet,
The scenes where so bravely thou'st lifted the blade,
Who have fought by thy side,
And remember thy pride,
When rushing to battle, with valour and ire,
Thou saw'st the fell foes of thy nation expire?

Can the warrior forget how sublimely you rose?
Like a star in the west,
When the sun's sink to rest,
That shines in bright splendour to dazzle our foes?
Thy arm and thy yell,
Once the tale could repel
Which slander invented, and minions detail,
And still shall thy actions refute the false tale.

Rest thou, noblest chief! in thy dark house of clay,
Thy deeds and thy name,
hy child's child shall proclaim,
And make the dark forests resound with the lay;
Though thy spirit has fled,
To the hills of the dead,
Yet thy name shall be held in my heart's warmest core,
And cherish'd till valour and love be no more.

自布鲁克林

依夫琳·斯科特[1]

沿着海岸
树枝犹如一张黑色的巨网
与淡黄色的路灯交织纠缠。
贝壳色的天空在夕阳下色彩斑斓。
曼哈顿漂浮在河的彼岸——
昏暗的灯火花园——
穿过暮霭无形地向我奔来，
人潮汹涌如飓风一般。

From Brooklyn

Evelyn Scott

Along the shore
A black net of branches
Tangles the pulpy yellow lamps.
The shell-colored sky is lustrous with the fading sun.
Across the river Manhattan floats—
Dim gardens of fire—
And rushing invisible toward me through the fog,
A hurricane of faces.

---

① 1893 ~ 1963，现代派代表人物之一。生于田纳西州，在路易斯安那州新奥尔良市长大，是美国20世纪二三十年代著名小说家、剧作家和诗人。

记忆之光

克拉克·阿什顿·史密斯[①]

岁月是一场降雪，
缓慢但不停歇，
覆盖丘陵、高山、鲜花和世界上的一切；
可是一时的激情
可以立即洗尽冲毁所有的积雪和长夜。
然而，云层缝隙中的
落日斜辉
以及隐约的山脉构成的崭新视野，
将西方变得峰回嶂叠
灵魂深处暖流涌射，
直到消融健忘之雪。

在记忆的长廊，
被久已遗忘的世界巅峰
直冲云霄永不下跌，
带着令人难以置信的重负，
立足于山岭牢固如铁。
凭借云层的巨大缝裂
我看到了一个广阔深邃的天地，
充满朦胧的暮色。

暮色空灵亮丽，犹如苍穹之上的超凡酒液，
在云层缝裂的下端变得醇厚浓烈，
生香活色。

---

① 1893 ~ 1961，美国西海岸知名诗人、小说家和雕塑家。生长于加利福尼亚州，初中毕业后因健康原因辍学，在家沉溺阅读和文学艺术创作。其文学作品具有奇幻的想象、宇宙的视野、华丽的词汇和嘲讽的诙谐。

Remembered Light

Clark Ashton Smith

The years are a falling of snow,
Slow, but without cessation,
On hills and mountains and flowers and worlds that were;
But snow and the crawling night in which it fell
May be washed away in one swifter hour of flame.
Thus it was that some slant of sunset
In the chasms of piled cloud—
Transient mountains that made a new horizon,
Uplifting the west to fantastic pinnacles—
Smote warm in a buried realm of the spirit,
Till the snows of forgetfulness were gone.

Clear in the vistas of memory,
The peaks of a world long unremembered,
Soared further than clouds, but fell not,
Based on hills that shook not nor melted
With that burden enormous, hardly to be believed.
Rent with stupendous chasms,
Full of an umber twilight,
I beheld that larger world.

Bright was the twilight, sharp like ethereal wine
Above, but low in the clefts it thickened,
Dull as with duskier tincture.

彩虹

埃菲·沃勒·史密斯[①]

天堂的阳光照亮尘世的泪珠
爱是一道彩虹
呈现在浩渺的苍穹。

光的所有不同色彩
都融会于那个美丽的弧拱：

在那里，激情的耀眼猩红
在真理的永恒湛蓝附近火光熊熊；

嫉妒的绿光
映照淫秽贪婪的金黄。

哦，如果没有那道爱的明亮彩虹，
黑暗的生活就像乌云笼罩的天空！

① 1879～1960，生于肯塔基州一个偏远山区农场，父母曾是奴隶。从一所黑人师范学校毕业后，她当过多年教师，业余从事诗歌创作，共出版三部诗集。

The Rainbow

Effie Waller Smith

Love is a rainbow that appears
When heaven's sunshine lights earth's tears.

All varied colors of the light
Within its beauteous arch unite:

There Passion's glowing crimson hue
Burns near Truth's rich and deathless blue;

And Jealousy's green lights unfold
‘Mid Pleasure's tints of flame and gold.

O dark life's stormy sky would seem,
If love's clear rainbow did not gleam!

之后

利奥诺拉·斯贝耶[①]

今晚我不会去林中漫步散心，
不会站在水边注目发愣
观看落日躺在黄昏的明亮边际
直到它抱着一颗星星，
默然西沉。

我不会去看黑暗蜿蜒的山岭
将我的悲伤慢慢围困，
我曾戴过山中轻轻枝叶的冠冕，
但如今群山犹如一个冷漠的蓝盾
压抑幽禁。

我不敢去面对那只欢唱的刀刃，
恣意地映照在夕阳下的松林，
明知我的渴求希冀，
仍用神的威力对我行刑，
直到鲜血淋淋。

无敌的鸟儿，请收起你的歌声，
不要用高亢的音符对我攻击欺凌，
怜悯，怜悯我吧，执着的鸟儿，
今晚我不想置身于你恐怖的
欢乐气氛。

---

① 1872～1956，职业小提琴演奏家，生于华盛顿特区一个贵族家庭，曾留学欧洲，在布鲁塞尔、巴黎和莱比锡学习音乐。42岁迁居纽约，开始诗歌创作，因诗集《小提琴手的告别》（*Fiddler's Farewell*）获1927年度普利策奖。

我害怕阴暗的森林，
我害怕诡异的树影，
隐藏在它们背后的记忆，
在那里时刻等着我，
入骨揪心。

After

Leonora Speyer

I will not walk in the wood to-night,
I will not stand by the water's edge
And see day lie on the dusk's bright ledge
Until it turn, a star at its breast,
To rest.

I will not see the wide-flung hills
Closing darkly about my grief,
I wore a crown of their lightest leaf,
But now they press like a cold, blue ring,
Imprisoning.

I dare not meet that caroling blade,
Jauntily drawn in the sunset pine,
Stabbing me with its thrust divine,
Knowing my naked, aching need,
Till I bleed.

Sheathe your song, invincible bird,
Strike not at me with that flashing note,
Have pity, have pity, persistent throat,
Deliver me not to your dread delight

To–night!

I am afraid of the creeping wood,
I am afraid of the furtive trees,
Hiding behind them, memories,
Ready to spring, to clutch, to tear,
Wait for me there.

夏悲

利奥诺拉·斯贝耶

广阔的鲜花草原有什么令我欢愉，
阵阵扩散的芬芳波浪，
寂静的的苔藓地衣怎样使我松弛，
或者夜风如何冷却我的渴望?
山岭，篱墙和云天，
回荡着我们的再见。

未摘的花蕾，抖动的绿叶，
小鸟发出一声无调的颤音，
溪流河水不安的梦幻之夜，
六月盛满的酒杯已洒泼殆尽——
你我的心是如此痴迷！——
夏天知道我们已经分离。

Summer Sorrow

Leonora Speyer

What shall meadow hold to please me,
Spreading wide its scented waving,
How shall quiet mosses ease me,
Or the night–wind cool my craving?
Hill and hedgerow, cloud–sweet sky,
Echo our good–by.

Bud unplucked and leaf a–quiver,
Bird that lifts a tuneless trilling,
Restless dream of brook and river,
All June's cup a wasted spilling—
You and I so thirsty–hearted!—
Summer knows us parted.

穿短裤的花农

华莱士·史蒂文斯[①]

我的鲜花被映照
在你的脑海
就像你被映照在你的杯中。
当你注视它们时，
你的脑海里只有
我的花的
倒影。
但是当我注视它们时
我唯一看见的
是你脑海里的反映，
而不是我的鲜花。
我期望
带着玫瑰，
来到你的面前
将它们放在一个白色的花盘里。

① 1879 ~ 1955，较有影响的现代派诗人。生于宾夕法尼亚州一个律师家庭，曾就读哈佛大学，毕业于纽约大学法学院，曾任保险公司高管。他业余从事诗歌创作，曾出版多部诗集。在哈佛就读时，他深受哲学家和文学家乔治·桑塔耶拿影响，成年后崇尚无神论哲学家和思想家弗里德里希·威廉·尼采。其诗歌作品风格独特，富有哲理。

The Florist Wears Knee-Breeches

Wallace Stevens

My flowers are reflected
In your mind
As you are reflected in your glass.
When you look at them,
There is nothing in your mind
Except the reflections
Of my flowers.
But when I look at them
I see only the reflections
In your mind,
And not my flowers.
It is my desire
To bring roses,
And place them before you
In a white dish.

秋季

伊丽莎白·德鲁·斯托达得[1]

这不是忧郁的季节!
　　看那日益多彩的枫叶,
橡树摇曳的倩影,
　　以及密密麻麻

藤蔓灌木丛的
　　猩红金黄颜色。
悲伤的皇冠
　　正从枝头飘落下跌。

带着露珠的草坪晶莹透亮,
　　林径路旁花毯相接。
星形紫菀和金黄的鼠尾草
　　纪录着秋天的每时每刻。

湛蓝的天空
　　白云如雪,
好像平静的银海波光粼粼
　　令人神怡心悦。

欢乐的气氛
　　让我兴高彩烈,
我披上亮丽的斗篷
　　去拥抱流逝的岁月。

---

① 1823 ~ 1902,小说家和诗人,生于马萨诸塞州一海滨小镇。其长篇小说深动刻画了19世纪末叶美国东海岸的社会生活,为现代主义和女权运动奠定了基础,在美国文学发展史上占有重要地位。她在报刊上发表的大量诗歌主要面向知识分子群体。

Autumn

Elizabeth Drew Stoddard

No melancholy days are these!
　　Not where the maple changing stands,
Not in the shade of fluttering oaks,
　　　　Nor in the bands

Of twisting vines and sturdy shrubs,
　　Scarlet and yellow, green and brown,
Falling, or swinging on their stalks,
　　　　Is Sorrow's crown.

The sparkling fields of dewy grass,
　　Woodpaths and roadsides decked with flowers,
Starred asters and the goldenrod,
　　　　Date Autumn's hours.

The shining banks of snowy clouds,
　　Steadfast in the aerial blue,
The silent, shimmering, silver sea,
　　　　To Joy are true.

My spirit in this happy air
　　Can thus embrace the dying year,
And with it wrap me in a shroud
　　　　As bright and clear!

春晨

马里恩·斯托贝尔[1]

哦，春天，我多么希望能将你捧在手心开怀畅饮，
让你这个闪亮的奇迹变成我身体的一部分！
哦，春天！
你将你的色彩在天空中旋转
直到我被美陶醉 颠倒神魂。
为什么我不能吸尽
所有光鲜的空气？
为什么寂静之中
能听到声音？
为什么每到这个时辰
会有感伤的歌声？
为什么没有花的时候
仍会闻到香水的清芬？
哦，春天！我怎么能与楚楚动人的你
靠得更近 更近？

① 1895 ~ 1967，诗人、小说家、文学评论家和《诗歌》杂志编辑，生于芝加哥一个土木工程师家庭。

Spring Morning

Marion Strobel

O day—if I could cup my hands and drink of you,
And make this shining wonder be A part of me!
O day! O day!
You lift and sway your colors on the sky
Till I am crushed with beauty.
Why is there
More of reeling sunlit air
Than I can breathe?
Why is there sound
In silence?
Why is a singing wound
About each hour?
And perfume when there is no flower?
O day! O Day! How may I press
Nearer to loveliness?

浩瀚时辰

吉拉维芙·塔格德①

夜幕降临，
白天的温暖甜蜜蒸发殆尽。
黑夜吞噬阳光，
世界归于沉静，
百灵的歌声伴随晌午碧草的芳香徐徐升腾。
神秘的翅翼划过天空，
群魔幽灵飘若浮云。
寂静的蜂房回荡着蜜蜂的嗡嗡低鸣，
在这缓慢凝重的时刻，我的思绪起伏难平。
只有三省吾身，
方可神闲意定。
在这浩瀚的时辰，光与黑暗相遇，
我的卷须沿树攀缘上升，
那里昏沉已经聚集，阴风蓄势出征。

① 1894 ~ 1948，生于华盛顿州一个教师家庭，两岁时随父母迁居夏威夷，13 岁开始写诗。在加利福尼亚大学伯克利分校读书时是一名活跃的社会主义者。大学毕业后前往纽约，曾在多所文理学院任教。其诗歌作品充分体现了她的政治社会观点。

The Vast Hour

Genevieve Taggard

All essences of sweetness from the white
Warm day go up in vapor, when the dark
Comes down. Ascends the tune of meadow–lark,
Ascends the noon–time smell of grass, when night
Takes sunlight from the world, and gives it ease.
Mysterious wings have brushed the air; and light
Float all the ghosts of sense and sound and sight;
The silent hive is echoing the bees.
So stir my thoughts at this slow, solemn time.
Now only is there certainty for me
When all the day's distilled and understood.
Now light meets darkness: now my tendrils climb
In this vast hour, up the living tree,
Where gloom foregathers, and the stern winds brood.

沙漠海子

莎拉·蒂斯黛尔[①]

我爱得过多；我是一条
　　充满泉水奔向大海的河，
我如此慷慨阔绰，
　　但是爱神不来惠顾捧喝。

他的双脚迈向沙漠
　　寸草不生雨露绝迹之所，
那里天空靛蓝冷酷
　　星星带着削尖的脸俯视闪烁。

午夜时分厌倦了长途奔波
　　他屈服于欲望之火
用污浊之水
　　去消解无法忍耐的干渴。

---

① 1884～1933，抒情诗人。生于密苏里州圣路易斯市，其诗集《情歌》荣获1918年度普利策奖。她因感情受挫罹患抑郁症而服毒自杀，年仅48岁。

Desert Pools

Sara Teasdale

I love too much; I am a river
  Surging with spring that seeks the sea,
I am too generous a giver,
  Love will not stoop to drink of me.

His feet will turn to desert places
  Shadowless, reft of rain and dew,
Where stars stare down with sharpened faces
  From heavens pitilessly blue.

And there at midnight sick with faring
  He will stoop down in his desire
To slake the thirst grown past all bearing
  In stagnant water keen as fire.

八月月升

莎拉·蒂斯黛尔

太阳已去，月亮升起
在蓝色的康州山脊；
东边嫣红，西面姹紫，
燕子在我头顶的上空
自由地飞来飞去。
我听到它们唧唧喳喳，看着它们敏捷飞驰
时而分开，时而聚集，
犹如黑色的花瓣从枝头飘落满地；
西边枫林的昏暗剪影
庄严静寂，
月亮正在慢慢升起
从朦胧的黄橙变成明亮的金橘
山岭越来越暗
从蔚蓝变成深紫。
我漫步下山，
却已忘乎所以，
因为夜晚湿润凉爽的清香，
令我无比欣喜
在一个闪光的水池边烂醉如泥。

哦，美神，我从小对你痴迷
你使我狂饮千杯
粗暴野蛮放荡不羁，
但是我现在终于确信无疑
没有任何苦楚可以阻挡
没有任何悲伤可以打击
一个人爱你到底。

如果我必须给予死神
我的每一次呼吸，
每一个笑意，
欢乐源泉的双眼，
和热情似火的丹赤；
假如一切都必须回归过去
沿着一条盲目而可怕的轨迹
使你能够重新开始，
与更剧烈的火焰融合，
成为更接近你渴望的东西；
如果我的灵魂必须孤独离去
穿过寒冷的极地，
甚至完全消失，
美神，我已顶礼膜拜过你。

让这个时辰来弥补
我的所有遗憾缺失。

August Moonrise

Sara Teasdale

The sun was gone, and the moon was coming
Over the blue Connecticut hills;
The west was rosy, the east was flushed,
And over my head the swallows rushed

This way and that, with changeful wills.
I heard them twitter and watched them dart
Now together and now apart
Like dark petals blown from a tree;
The maples stamped against the west
Were black and stately and full of rest,
And the hazy orange moon grew up
And slowly changed to yellow gold
While the hills were darkened, fold on fold
To a deeper blue than a flower could hold.
Down the hill I went, and then
I forgot the ways of men,
For night–scents, heady, and damp and cool
Wakened ecstasy in me
On the brink of a shining pool.

O Beauty, out of many a cup
You have made me drunk and wild
Ever since I was a child,
But when have I been sure as now
That no bitterness can bend
And no sorrow wholly bow

One who loves you to the end?
And though I must give my breath
And my laughter all to death,
And my eyes through which joy came,
And my heart, a wavering flame;
If all must leave me and go back
Along a blind and fearful track
So that you can make anew,
Fusing with intenser fire,
Something nearer your desire;
If my soul must go alone
Through a cold infinity,
Or even if it vanish, too,
Beauty, I have worshipped you.

Let this single hour atone
For the theft of all of me.

神谕者

莎拉·蒂斯黛尔

我将重新振作自己，
　　将散乱的自我拾起聚集
融合成一个抛光的水晶球
　　让我能够洞察日月天地。

我将时刻专注地坐着，像一个女巫，
　　观察未来光临和现在离去，
以及人潮涌动忙碌
　　焦虑不安踌躇满志。

The Crystal Gazer

Sara Teasdale

I shall gather myself into myself again,
　　I shall take my scattered selves and make them one,
Fusing them into a polished crystal ball
　　Where I can see the moon and the flashing sun.

I shall sit like a sibyl, hour after hour intent,
　　Watching the future come and the present go,
And the little shifting pictures of people rushing
　　In restless self-importance to and fro.

晨歌

莎拉·蒂斯黛尔

一缕闪亮的曙光
　　将我从梦中唤醒；
黎明已经吞噬了星星
　　只留下白月的残影。

哦，白月，你是那么孤寂，
　　我也离索如此，
但是我们可以漫游世界，
　　只有孤独者才自由无拘。

Morning Song

Sara Teasdale

A diamond of a morning
　　Waked me an hour too soon;
Dawn had taken in the stars
　　And left the faint white moon.

O white moon, you are lonely,
　　It is the same with me,
But we have the world to roam over,
　　Only the lonely are free.

冬眠

爱迪思·玛蒂尔达·托马斯[1]

我知道一定到了冬天，
我知道一定到了冬天，因为我梦想
将赤脚放进清泉，
鲜花遍地，芳草满甸。

我知道自己一定老了，
我知道自己一定老了，因为无意之中
我的心变得年轻，犹如秋天的原野回光返照
晚雨浇灌垂落的枯草。

我知道自己已经身心疲惫，
我知道自己已经身心疲惫，因为我的灵魂
从冒险中得到安慰，
犹如风暴将松林变成交响乐队。

我知道自己正在走向死亡，
我知道自己正在走向死亡，因为我渴望生命
顽强的生命，而非坟场，
和寒霜中寂静的山岗。

① 1854～1925，最著名的美国诗人之一。生于俄亥俄州，毕业于当地一所师范学校。青年时代迁居纽约，担任期刊编辑并从事写作，在报刊上发表三百余首诗歌。

Winter Sleep

Edith Matilda Thomas

I know it must be winter (though I sleep)—
I know it must be winter, for I dream
I dip my bare feet in the running stream,
And flowers are many, and the grass grows deep.

I know I must be old (how age deceives!)
I know I must be old, for, all unseen,
My heart grows young, as autumn fields grow green
When late rains patter on the falling sheaves.

I know I must be tired (and tired souls err)—
I know I must be tired, for all my soul
To deeds of daring beats a glad, faint roll,
As storms the riven pine to music stir.

I know I must be dying (Death draws near)—
I know I must be dying, for I crave Life—
life, strong life, and think not of the grave,
And turf–bound silence, in the frosty year.

太阳颂

埃洛伊兹·比伯·汤普森[①]

哦，太阳，多少地方，
你还没有照亮！
哦，阳光，多少眼泪，
在的面前已经流淌！
你的耀眼光芒怎能知道
痛心的悲怆，
刺耳的哀嚎，
以及世态炎凉！
悲伤的标枪，
刺破了多少心脏？
激情的豪雨，
令无数的大脑疯狂。
绝望的利刃，
将忧郁的众生戕伤。
难道你高高在上
视若无睹 习以为常？
照耀吧，雄伟的太阳！
照耀吧，辉煌的太阳！
你的灿烂光芒，
给我灰暗枯躁的生活
带来快乐希望。
你的奇妙之光，
是我每天感受的关爱
温暖安详。

① 1878 ~ 1928，记者、剧作家和诗人。生于新奥尔良一个黑人中产阶层家庭，曾就读新奥尔良大学，成为一名教师。后毕业于霍华德大学，并在哥伦比亚大学和纽约大学进修。大学毕业后弃教从文。婚后与丈夫诺亚·汤普森迁居洛杉矶，夫妻俩都是当地“喷墨机”（Ink Slingers）文学团体的活跃成员。

Ode to the Sun

Eloise Bibb Thompson

How many scenes, O sun,
Hast thou not shone upon!
How many tears, O light,
Have dropped before thy sight!
How many heart–felt sighs,
How many piercing cries,
How many deeds of woe,
Dost thy bright light not know!
How many broken hearts,
That are pierced by sorrow's darts
How many maddened brains,
That are wild with passion's rains;
How many soul–sick lives,
Stabbed with despair's sharp knives,
Hast thou above the skies,
Not seen with thy radiant eyes!
Shine on, majestic one!
Shine on, O glorious sun!
And never fail to cheer
My life so dark and drear.
Whene'er thou shinest bright,
And show thy brilliant light,
The cares I know each day
Silently steal away.

月亮之歌

普莉希拉·简·汤普森[1]

哦，我的胸膛有股隐藏的力量，
　　这股力量无人能够想象；
我从平静的大海中呼唤潮汐，
大海便按我的旨意潮落潮涨；
很多迟钝渔民的木船
被我破肚开膛，残渣碎片
　　在汹涌的潮汐中随波逐浪。

我是一个巫婆，歹毒心肠；
　　暗地里我操纵风雨气象；
我的光芒中有一股神奇的力量，
能在情人的心中点燃欲望，
我也能寻找亡者的灵魂，
从沼泽中召唤海潮巨浪，
　　让欲望和灵魂一起随波飘荡。

我从山巅召唤雨神，
　　让巨雷滚滚作响；
我周而复始消长，
天堂错乱无章，人们徒劳地寻找
破解我所拥有的神奇力量，
但是我只展现了有限的一部分，
　　人们只好冥思苦想。

① 1871 ~ 1942，生于俄亥俄州，其父母是从弗吉尼亚州逃亡辛辛那提的奴隶。她从师范学校毕业后，因心脏病无法正常工作，便在家从事写作并在当地教堂和学校朗读自己创作的诗歌。其诗歌赞颂黑人妇女的智慧和美丽，激发了哈莱姆黑人文艺复兴运动。

是的，无人知晓我暗中的坚强；
　　也无人理解我的神奇力量；
我能制造涌流的潮水波浪，
我会残缺，也会盈满，
人类绞尽脑汁，
对我的奥秘仍然破解无方，
　　他徒劳地寻找，困惑迷惘。

Song of the Moon

Priscilla Jane Thompson

Oh, a hidden power is in my breast,
　　A power that none can fathom;
I call the tides from seas of rest,
They rise, they fall, at my behest;
And many a tardy fisher's boat,
I've torn apart and set afloat,
　　From out their raging chasm.

For I'm an enchantress, old and grave;
　　Concealed I rule the weather;
Oft set I, the lover's heart a blaze,
With hidden power of my fulgent rays,
Or seek I the souls of dying men,
And call the sea-tides from the fen,
　　And drift them out together.

I call the rain from the mountain's peak,
　　And sound the mighty thunder;
When I wax and wane from week to week,
The heavens stir, while vain men seek,

To solve the myst'ries that I hold,
But a bounded portion I unfold,
    So nations pass and wonder.

Yea, my hidden strength no man may know;
    Nor myst'ries be expounded;
I'll cause the tidal waves to flow,
And I shall wane, and larger grow,
Yet while man rack his shallow brain,
The secrets with me still remain,
    He seeks in vain, confounded.

独处

欧文·W. 昂德希尔[1]

哦，独处，哪里是你的刺痛，
　　人们对你如此形容？
哪里是你的恐怖面孔？
　　我四处寻找，但是无影无踪。

哪里隐藏着你的寂寞，
　　世界自诩对你的畏惧和惶恐？
躺在你充满爱的怀抱里，
　　我感到其乐融融。

不，他们对你一无所知，
　　他们只是白痴盲从。
否则他们会识别你的真容，
　　尊贵的大自然教育之母。

因为你的惠顾，在典籍之中，
　　古老的吟游诗人和先哲前贤，
成为与我倾心交流的高朋，
　　他们的真知灼见光彩夺目。

生命中的疑问和困惑
　　令我迷惘朦胧，
我知道，哦，独处，
　　答案在冥思默想之中。

---

① 1868～1950，黑人诗人，生于宾夕法尼亚州中部小镇克林顿港。1916年诗集《爸爸的爱》出版。

我的心充满了悲痛，
　　难以承受哀伤与惊恐，
哦，独处，在你的臂膀之中
　　我得到抚慰疏通。

我厌倦了世上的
　　欺诈和肆虐逞凶，
在你的身上我发现甜美的静谧
　　和新生命的兴荣。

完美的花园里，
　　不能没有玫瑰盛开的芳容。
我的生命中，
　　不能缺少独处宁静的轻松。

Solitude

Irvin W. Underhill

Oh, solitude, where is the sting,
　　That men ascribe to thee?
Where is the terror in thy mien?
　　I look, but cannot see.

Where hidest thou, that loneliness
　　The world pretends to fear?
While lying on thy loving breast
　　I find my sweetest cheer.

They do not understand thee, no,
　　They are but knaves or fools,
Or else they must discern in thee
　　Dame Nature's queen of schools.

For in thy care, with naught but books,
　　The bards and saints of old,
Become my friends and to mine ear
　　Their mystic truths unfold.

When problems and perplexities
　　Of life becloud my mind,
I know in thee, oh, solitude,
　　The answer I can find.

When grief and sorrow crowd my heart
　　To breaking, with their fears
Within thy arms, oh, solitude,
　　I find relief in tears.

And when I weary of the world's
　　Deceits and cares and strife,
I find in thee sweet rest and peace
　　And vigorous new life.

My garden never is complete
　　Without a blooming rose,
Nor is my life, oh, solitude,
　　Without thy sweet repose.

冬寄春

欧文·W. 昂德希尔

我不曾记得我的头发花白
　　而且所剩无几，
但我仍会追随你的脚步走来
　　从黎明直到月落星稀。

你的双眼犹如喜悦和青春的源泉
　　令我想起早已逝去的光阴，
我的爱人，我走向真理的圣殿，
　　得到的却是欢乐之春。

如今冬天随着风雪而至
　　使我如同树林一样光秃裸露，
哦，是的，我依然爱你，但只在心里，
　　因为我的双膝变得软弱无助。

你的言语如小鸟的歌声一样甜蜜，
　　你的举止堪比幼鹿的优雅温驯，
我在梦中想你，亲爱的——哦，请原谅我用这个词，
　　从黄昏直到黎明。

你将无法在这封信的开端找到你的名字，
　　我也不会在信的结尾署名，
因为冬天必须默默承受极乐悲喜
为了所爱的芳春。

Winter to Spring

Irwin W. Underhill

Did not I remember that my hair is grey
With only a fringe of it left,
I'd follow your footsteps from wee break of day
Till night was of moon-light bereft.

Your eyes wondrous fountains of joy and of youth
Remind me of days long since flown,
My sweetheart, I led to the altar of truth,
But then the gay spring was my own.

Now winter has come with its snow and its wind
And made me as bare as its trees,
Oh, yes, I still love, but it's only in mind,
For I'm fast growing weak at the knees.

Your voice is as sweet as the song of a bird,
Your manners are those of the fawn,
I dream of you, darling,—oh, pardon, that word,
From twilight to breaking of dawn.

Your name in this missive you'll search for in vain,
Nor mine at the finis, I'll fling,
For winter must suffer the bliss and the pain
In secret for loving the spring.

冬鸟

琼斯·瓦雷[1]

你站在冬天光秃的树枝上独自歌唱，
好像身着盛装的春姑娘就在你的身旁；
她的欢笑在溪水中流淌，
她的细语随着微风飘过草原山岗，
你听见她轻轻地
加入你阵阵嘹亮的声浪。
唱吧，尽管她的甜美被疾风淹没，
尽管你的歌声被暴雪遗忘，
然而她的音乐唤醒了我的心，
以及一个至亲的念想；
虽然溪流可能冻结，虽然她会变得沉默，
虽然草原上的劲风不再躁狂，
但是我听到你的快乐歌声，
我依然觉得，我年暮的心可以像你一样欢唱。

① 1813～1880，神职人员和诗人及超验主义运动先驱，生于马萨诸塞州一个海滨小镇，曾就读哈佛大学神学院。他潜心莎士比亚研究，其诗歌带有浓郁的莎士比亚十四行诗风格。

The Winter Bird

Jones Very

Thou sing'st alone on the bare wintry bough,
As if Spring with its leaves were around thee now;
And its voice that was heard in the laughing rill,
And the breeze as it whispered o'er meadow and hill,
Still fell on thine ear, as it murmured along
To join the sweet tide of thine own gushing song.
Sing on—though its sweetness was lost on the blast,
And the storm has not heeded thy song as it passed,
Yet its music awoke in a heart that was near,
A thought whose remembrance will ever prove dear;
Though the brook may be frozen, though silent its voice,
And the gales through the meadows no longer rejoice,
Still I felt, as my ear caught thy glad note of glee,
That my heart in life's winter might carol like thee.

印第安人情歌

伯川德·N. O. 沃克[①]

小屋灯光闪烁，我多么爱你，
小屋灯光闪烁，我多么爱你，
　　麦安萨，我的森林小鹿！
为了目睹你路过时的倩影，
　　我在黎明时的山顶久久徘徊不愿离去。

天边曙光初现，我多么爱你，
天边曙光初现，我多么爱你！
　　你跋涉在通往春天的陡峭山路，
　　我将木笛弃之于地，
你的出现使我的歌声戛然而止。

河上缕缕月光，
湖上点点星光！
　　月光和星光不足挂齿，
　　因为它们永远不能
与你眼中流露的爱光相比。

① 1870～1927，生于俄克拉何马州一个印地安人部落，在密苏里州印地安人学校和公立学校接受教育。成年后一直从事怀安多特族儿童的教育工作，并出版了两部反映印地安人生活风俗的诗集。

An Indian Love Song

Bertrand N. O. Walker

Light o' the lodge, how I love thee,
Light o' the lodge, how I love thee,
Mianza, my wild–wood fawn!
To wait and to watch for thy passing.
On hill–top I linger at dawn.

Glimmer of morn, how I love thee,
Glimmer of morn, how I love thee!
My flute to the ground now I fling,
As you tread the steep trail to the spring,
For thy coming has silenced my song.

Shimmer of moon on the river,
Sheen of soft star on the lake!
Moonlight and starlight are naught;
Their gleam and their glow is ne'er fraught
With such love–light as falls from thine eyes.

莫哈韦摇篮曲

伯川德·N. O. 沃克

睡吧，我的小男孩，
做梦的时刻已经到来。

在牧豆树
密密麻麻的枝丫中，
鸟妈妈已将她的小宝宝
偎抱于怀；看啦
山中游动着你祖先的魂骸，
青黛的阴影向东爬来，
从西边苍白的天际
夜幕徐徐拉开。

东边的山岭一片明亮，
看啦，尖尖的峰顶晚霞犹如火海，
闪烁着伟大的苍天酋长
赐予你父亲的弓箭色彩。
嘘，我的小男孩；不要害怕
你的爸爸马上就回来。
在河边的小径上，
高密的荆棘杂草
将你爸爸的黑发掩盖，看啦
他用有力的双手将它们分开，
快步向家走来。
他即将回到妈妈身边，
见到家中的妈妈和小男孩。

睡吧，我的小乖乖，
白天已经不在。
枝头的小鸟停止了唧唧喳喳，
做梦的时刻已经到来。

A Mojave Lullaby

Bertrand N.O. Walker

Sleep, my little man–child,
Dream–time to you has come.

In the closely matted branches
Of the mesquite tree,
The mother–bird has nestled
Her little ones; see
From the ghost–hills of your fathers,
Purpling shadows eastward crawl,
While beyond the western sky–tints pale
As twilight spreads its pall.

The eastern hills are lighted,
See their sharp peaks burn and glow,
With the colors the Great Sky–Chief
Gave your father for his bow.
Hush my man–child; be not frighted,
'Tis the father's step draws nigh.
O'er the trail along the river,
Where the arrow–weeds reach high
Above his dark head, see
He parts them with his strong hands,
As he steps forth into view.

He is coming home to mother,
Home to mother and to you.

Sleep my little man–child,
Daylight has gone.
There's no twitter in the branches,
Dream–time has come.

窗台上的鲜花

卢西安·B. 沃特金斯[①]

啊，我的心是如此欢畅，我以轻快的脚步奔忙
　　终日劳作在亲爱的家乡；
我将告诉你是什么让我的生活变得如此明亮——
　　我的窗台上有朵鲜花正在旺盛开放。

它在阳光下流金溢彩，阵雨过后更是喜气洋洋；
　　它在空气中散发着甜蜜的芬芳。
它实在可爱！愿它的美丽永不消亡——
　　这朵亲爱的鲜花盛开在我的窗台上。

大自然给它穿上如此华丽的衣裳，
　　让我们的家充满快乐吉祥，让我们的心透彻明亮；
尽管它会凋谢，对它亲切的记忆我将今生不忘——
　　这朵亲爱的鲜花盛开在我的窗台上。

我常常凝视这朵盛开的鲜花，它的花瓣洁白明亮。
　　我看到它的霓裳，我不禁联想
在人生旅程中，但愿我们所有人的生活充满快乐 远离忧伤
　　就像这朵鲜花盛开在我的窗台上。

---

① 1879 ~ 1921，非裔诗人和教师。生于弗吉尼亚州，曾在军队服役并参加第一次世界大战。1903 年其诗集《寂静之声》出版。

The Flower at My Window

Lucian B. Watkins

O! my heart now feels so cheerful as I go with footsteps light
In the daily toil of my dear home;
And I'll tell to you the secret that now makes my life so bright—
There's a flower at my window in full bloom.

It is radiant in the sunshine, and so cheerful after rain;
And it wafts upon the air its sweet perfume.
It is very, very lovely! May its beauties never wane—
This dear flower at my window in full bloom.

Nature has so clothed it in such glorious array,
And it does so cheer our home, and hearts illume;
Its dear mem'ry I will cherish though the flower fade away—
This dear flower at my window in full bloom.

Oft I gaze upon this flower with its blossoms pure and white.
And I think as I behold its gay costume,
While through life we all are passing may our lives be always bright
Like this flower at my window in full bloom.

双视角

卢西安 · B. 沃特金斯

从低矮的平原仰看；
哦，生活
是多么甜蜜恬静美好，我不禁感叹，
在那高山的顶部是一个金色的皇冠！

从巨大高耸的山体鸟瞰：
那脚下的平原百合灿烂
多么明亮安祥青翠温暖！

Two Points of View

Lucian B. Watkins

From this low-lying valley;
Oh, how sweet And cool and calm and great is life, I ween,
There on yon mountain-throne—that sun-gold crest!

From this uplifted, mighty mountain-seat:
How bright and still and warm and soft and green
Seems yon low lily-vale of peace and rest!

流亡

威尼弗雷德·威尔斯[1]

我已将悲伤变成一种华贵的东西，
将忧郁当作一种特殊的服饰。
我用大如星斗的泪珠装扮我的发髻，
我的沉默像令人惊叹的蓝宝石戒指。
哦，黑暗比任何光更能让我
散发一种特有的魅力，
阴影带来的珍珠般高贵
胜于我能穿的任何玉帛锦衣。
还有什么能让我这样的人欣喜？
黄昏已是如此瑰丽
黎明还能为我带来怎样的神奇？
笑声将回荡在天空里——
我将无冕而立，远离这动乱的尘世，
衣衫褴褛，抛弃一切，放逐天际。

---

① 1893～1939，作家和编辑。成长于康涅狄格州，婚后与丈夫哈罗德·希勒迁居纽约市，曾与诗人埃里诺·伟丽为邻。曾发表五部诗集，其第一部诗集《迟疑的心》（*The Hesitant Heart*）受到较高评价。其诗作以浓烈的情感和细腻描述著称。

Exile

Winifred Welles

I have made grief a gorgeous, queenly thing,
And worn my melancholy with an air.
My tears were big as stars to deck my hair,
My silence stunning as a sapphire ring.
Oh, more than any light the dark could fling
A glamour over me to make me rare,
Better than any color I could wear
The pearly grandeur that the shadows bring.
What is there left to joy for such as I?
What throne can dawn upraise for me who found
The dusk so royal and so rich a one?
Laughter will whirl and whistle on the sky—
Far from this riot I shall stand uncrowned,
Disrobed, bereft, an outcast in the sun.

感恩

艾拉·惠勒·威尔科克斯[①]

漫步在争妍斗艳的花园草地
　　我们不会关注那些平凡的雏菊；
对于常见的恩赐
　　我们很少赞美感激。
我们感叹某些给我们的生命
　　增添辉煌的极乐喜事，
然而忽略日常生活中的
　　温馨甜蜜。

我们的担忧无所不及
　　以致影响我们的思维感知。
我们每天的光阴
　　正是享乐之时。
然而我们却浪费和忘记
　　那么多唾手可得的欣喜。
如果我们让忧虑征服
　　我们的生活将被郁闷充斥。

一年之中的每一日
　　都隐藏着某些喜悦乐趣。
然而蓦然回首，欢乐常常出现在
　　过去的边缘缝隙。

---

① 1850 ~ 1919，素食主义者和动物权利倡导者。生于威斯康星州一个知识分子家庭，8 岁开始写诗，高中毕业时已是当地颇有名气的诗人。其诗歌使用大众化语言表达强烈的情感，深受读者喜爱。

我相信，恩赐就像我们身边的
　　亲情和友谊，
我们应当高声赞美，
　　跳动的心脏尚未停止。

很多恩赐
　　都戴着忧虑或烦恼的面具；
智者的远见卓识
　　洞知悲喜相依。
他凭借信仰和毅力
　　怀着悲痛感谢上帝
因为他找到了圣洁的快乐
　　用它去欢度每一个明日。

我们应该感激
　　每一个幸福的记忆和恩赐；
以及生命乐章中
　　停顿休止期的每时每日。
只有这样，我们漫长的人生岁月
　　才会奏响高亢的主旋律。
恢宏的感恩大合唱
　　将响起在这个美好的日子里。

Thanksgiving

Ella Wheeler Wilcox

We walk on starry fields of white
    And do not see the daisies;
For blessings common in our sight
    We rarely offer praises.
We sigh for some supreme delight
    To crown our lives with splendor,
And quite ignore our daily store
    Of pleasures sweet and tender.

Our cares are bold and push their way
    Upon our thought and feeling.
They hand about us all the day,
    Our time from pleasure stealing.
So unobtrusive many a joy
    We pass by and forget it,
But worry strives to own our lives,
    And conquers if we let it.

There's not a day in all the year
    But holds some hidden pleasure,
And looking back, joys oft appear
    To brim the past's wide measure.
But blessings are like friends, I hold,
    Who love and labor near us.
We ought to raise our notes of praise
    While living hearts can hear us.

Full many a blessing wears the guise
Of worry or of trouble;
Far–seeing is the soul, and wise,
Who knows the mask is double.
But he who has the faith and strength
To thank his God for sorrow
Has found a joy without alloy
To gladden every morrow.

We ought to make the moments notes
Of happy, glad Thanksgiving;
The hours and days a silent phrase
Of music we are living.
And so the theme should swell and grow
As weeks and months pass o'er us,
And rise sublime at this good time,
A grand Thanksgiving chorus.

新年

艾拉·惠勒·威尔科克斯

有什么新年寄语，
还没有被说一千次？

新年来，旧年去，
我们知道我们梦想，我们梦想我们所知。

早晨起床我们带着笑意，
晚上躺下我们默默哭泣。

我们拥抱世界直到被它蜇刺，
我们诅咒世界感叹时光流逝。

我们生活，我们珍惜，我们求爱，我们嫁娶，
我们给新娘戴上花环，我们给死者穿上寿衣。

我们欢笑，我们痛哭，我们希望，我们恐惧，
这便是一年的重负与天职。

The Year

Ella Wheeler Wilcox

What can be said in New Year rhymes,
That's not been said a thousand times?

The new years come, the old years go,
We know we dream, we dream we know.

We rise up laughing with the light,
We lie down weeping with the night.

We hug the world until it stings,
We curse it then and sigh for wings.

We live, we love, we woo, we wed,
We wreathe our brides, we sheet our dead.

We laugh, we weep, we hope, we fear,
And that's the burden of the year.

露珠

麦拉·维尔拉·魏尔慈[1]

瞧，晨露滴滴，
　　犹如一粒粒晃动的钻石，
躺在静静的小床里，
　　璀璨发亮，光彩熠熠。

看！芳草萋萋，
　　在晨露的滋润下根繁叶密；
让我们像露珠一样，
　　沿途散发爱的宝石。

Dewdrops

Myra Viola Wilds

Watch the dewdrops in the morning,
　　Shake their little diamond heads,
Sparkling, flashing, ever moving,
　　From their silent little beds.

See the grass! Each blade is brightened,
　　Roots are strengthened by their stay;
Like the dewdrops, let us scatter
　　Gems of love along the way.

① 生卒年月不详，非裔妇女，生长于肯塔基州。她自幼失明，未接受过学校教育，以缝纫制衣为生，其诗集《空闲时光的随想》于 1915 年出版。

理想

麦拉·维尔拉·魏尔慈

你带着怎样的理想
　　在日常旅行中
它们是崇高明亮，
　　还是卑微迷茫？

重要的不是它们百般花样，
　　或者你是怎样的神工巧匠；
你也许位高权重，
　　但最宝贵的还是你的理想。

紧紧抓住你的理想，
　　让它们焕发荣光；
将它们锻造洗涤擦亮，
　　然后让它们在爱中自由飞翔。

Thoughts

Myra Viola Wilds

What kind of thoughts now, do you carry
In your travels day by day
Are they bright and lofty visions,
Or neglected, gone astray?

Matters not how great in fancy,
Or what deeds of skill you've wrought;
Man, though high may be his station,
Is no better than his thoughts.

Catch your thoughts and hold them tightly,
Let each one an honor be;
Purge them, scourge them, burnish brightly,
Then in love set each one free.

人生

埃玛·劳里·威廉姆斯[①]

我们无法预知
世上有怎样的幸福和欣喜。
如果心无旁骛
终会不断进取。
罪恶的弊端一览无余
对于他人以及我们自己。
我们可能枉度漫长的一生，
拥有很多宝贵的东西却抱怨不止。
也许在别人眼里，
我们非常富有和睿智；
但是如果我们内心不善，
人生将不会灿烂美丽。
哦！愿我们的生命日复一日
在爱和责任中流逝；
最后我们的躯体消亡，
仍然可以活在天国里；
那里没有罪恶，死亡和痛苦，
好人将会相爱重聚。

---

① 1834～？，印地安人后裔，毕业于俄克拉何马州切诺基女子学校，终身投入印地安部落儿童教育工作，是美国最早出自印地安部落的女诗人之一。

Life

Emma Lowrey Williams

We can not tell what happiness
We might on earth possess
If in singleness of heart
We would strive to act a proper part.
'Tis true we see the effects of sin
All without and all within.
We long may live a life in vain,
Much good possess, but still complain.
We may appear to other eyes,
To be extremely rich and wise;
But if our hearts are not right,
Life will not be beautiful and bright.
Oh! may our life, day by day,
In love and duty pass away;
And at last when our bodies die,
We may live in that world above the sky;
Where free from sin, death and pain,
The good will meet and love again.

灰色画像

威廉·卡罗斯·威廉姆斯[①]

难道永远不可能
将你和你的灰色分开？
难道你必须总是融合于
灰褐色的背景——远方的树总是映衬着灰色的天空？

难道我必须
总是与你逆向而动？
难道没有地方
在那里我们可以存异求同和平与共？

我看见自己
站在你的肩上
触摸灰色破碎的天空——
而你不堪重负，却紧紧抓着我的脚踝
在未被颜色搅乱的平整之处
艰难向前移动。

① 1883 ~ 1963，出生于新泽西州一个加勒比海移民家庭，父亲来自多米尼加，母亲来自波多黎各。他毕业于宾夕法尼亚大学医学院，是一名儿科医生。他白天行医，晚上写作，是一名多产作家和颇有影响的印象派和现代派诗人。

A Portrait in Greys

William Carlos Williams

Will it never be possible
to separate you from your greyness?
Must you be always sinking backward
into your grey-brown landscapes—and trees
always in the distance, always against a grey sky?

Must I be always
moving counter to you? Is there no place
where we can be at peace together
and the motion of our drawing apart
be altogether taken up?
I see myself
standing upon your shoulders touching
a grey, broken sky—
but you, weighted down with me,
yet gripping my ankles,—move
laboriously on,
where it is level and undisturbed by colors.

月光

伊沃·温特斯[1]

我等待
在深秋的月光，
思绪的列车嗡嗡作响——

心思月光
联翩浮想。

犹如一丝流过寒夜的溪水
迷茫彷徨，
孤独超越寂寞惆怅

将这首歌轻轻唱给孩子们，
伴随怀旧的听众进入梦乡，

没有守护者
跨越千里奔忙，
他的眼睛是一张无形的篷帐。

---

① 1900～1968，当代活跃且具影响力的文学评论家，生于芝加哥，曾就读芝加哥大学。大学期间开始诗歌创作。因患结核病辍学去新墨西哥州圣达菲疗养，毕业于科罗拉多大学，获文学艺术学士和硕士学位。因年轻时在美国西南部多年的生活经历，早年作品深受印地安人语言文化影响，对20世纪初叶意象派诗歌的发展影响显著。26岁时入斯坦福大学攻读文学博士学位，毕业后留校任教，培养了一批著名诗人。攻读博士学位期间，对西方文学艺术，特别是英国传统诗歌的韵律学，进行了系统研究，从而促进其作品风格从意象派到现代派的转变。发表了大量诗歌，主张作品不能仅局限于个人观感及浪漫情怀，而应遵守既定的韵律格式并给予读者清新的见解和体验。

The Moonlight

Yvor Winters

I waited on
In the late autumn moonlight,
A train droning out of thought—

The mind on moonlight
And on trains.

Blind as a thread of water
Stirring through a cold like dust,
Lonely beyond all silence

And humming this to children,
The nostalgic listeners in sleep,

Because no guardian
Strides through distance upon distance,
His eyes a web of sleep.

雨铃

埃里诺·伟丽[①]

梦神来临，伴随清澈的雨滴，
落在镇上陡峭的崖壁。
梦神来临，人们重新安息
雨点轻轻飘落于地。

明亮的雨滴声像玻璃铃一样清晰
在微风中娓娓依稀；
与其沉眠于宁静的草地
不如酣睡在坚硬的岩石。

逝者对于和平的到来毫不在意；
长眠中，他们可以享受无限的安息。
生者血淋淋的头颅，
窃以为，对和平最珍惜。

① 1885～1928，生于新泽西州一个名门望族，祖父曾任宾夕法尼亚州州长。她从小在华盛顿特区的贵族学校接受教育，天生丽质，才华出众，成为引人注目的社交名媛。诗歌深受英国浪漫主义影响，语言简洁生动，表达深刻细腻，其诗集《捕风之网》在美国文学界评价很高。

Bells in the Rain

Elinor Wylie

Sleep falls, with limpid drops of rain,
Upon the steep cliffs of the town.
Sleep falls; men are at peace again
While the small drops fall softly down.

The bright drops ring like bells of glass
Thinned by the wind; and lightly blown;
Sleep cannot fall on peaceful grass
So softly as it falls on stone.

Peace falls unheeded on the dead
Asleep; they have had deep peace to drink;
Upon a live man's bloody head
It falls most tenderly, I think.

丝绒鞋

埃里诺·伟丽

让我们去雪中漫游
　　在无声的空间里；
迈着轻缓的脚步行走，
　　随着安宁的步履
　　戴着面纱和白色蕾丝。

我将穿上丝绸鞋，
　　而你踏着羊毛屐，
洁白如牛奶，
　　比海鸥的腹羽
　　更美丽。

我们将走过沉寂的镇市
　　在无风的宁静中；
我们踏着白色的鹅羽，
　　踏着银色的羊绒，
　　踏着比这些更柔软的轻空。

我们将穿着丝绒鞋步行：
　　无论我们走到何处
安谧将如露水降临
　　于脚下白色的静物。
　　我们将在雪中漫步。

Velvet Shoes

Elinor Wylie

Let us walk in the white snow
        In a soundless space;
With footsteps quiet and slow,
        At a tranquil pace,
        Under veils of white lace.

I shall go shod in silk,
        And you in wool,
White as white cow's milk,
        More beautiful
        Than the breast of a gull.

We shall walk through the still town
        In a windless peace;
We shall step upon white down,
        Upon silver fleece,
        Upon softer than these.

We shall walk in velvet shoes:
        Wherever we go
Silence will fall like dews
        On white silence below.
        We shall walk in the snow.

逃 避

埃里诺·伟丽

狐狸吃掉最后一粒金黄的葡萄，
最后一只白色的羚羊残遭杀戮，
我会停止战斗而逃跑
到我即将建造的一个小屋。

但是首先我会变成精灵模样，
用一种无人能懂的魔咒，
将你们所有的眼睛变成失明的月亮，
将你们所有的双手变成泥泞的道路。

你们会徒劳地将我寻找
在红树根的空洞，
或者在银色的蜂巢，
像水果一样垂挂在带有苹果香味的雨中。

Escape

Elinor Wylie

When foxes eat the last gold grape,
And the last white antelope is killed,

I shall stop fighting and escape
Into a little house I'll build.
But first I'll shrink to fairy size,
With a whisper no one understands,
Making blind moons of all your eyes,

And muddy roads of all your hands.
And you may grope for me in vain
In hollows under the mangrove root,
Or where, in apple–scented rain,
The silver wasp–nests hang like fruit.

后 记

《永恒的美丽——美国平民诗选》的出版是一系列机缘巧合的结果。三年前开始从事翻译的动机仅仅是为了练习中文。来美国求学和工作转眼三十余年，长期生活在英语环境里，平时很少使用母语，中文慢慢变得生疏。加上年龄增长，记忆力逐渐减退，连许多常用汉字的书写也开始遗忘。为了减缓这种语言上的废用性萎缩，我决定尝试每周利用业余时间将一两首美国诗歌译成中文，不仅有利于学习两种语言，还可自娱自乐，甚至发在微信群里与亲友分享。原计划将这项练习持续一年，但不久新冠肺炎疫情在全球暴发，开始长期的居家隔离和远程办公生活。作为一名流行病学专业人员，世纪大瘟疫对我的工作负担和心理压力影响巨大。而研读和翻译诗歌自然成为我缓解疲劳和焦虑的有效措施。这项周末例行练习因此一直持续到现在。

在与亲友们分享这些译作的过程中，我收到很多诚恳的建议和热情鼓励。其中一些亲友极力推荐将这些诗歌结集出版，介绍给更多读者。我长年生活在海外，对国内的出版行业一无所知。托国内朋友打听联系出版社均无功而返。年前偶尔与华中科技大学同济医学院陈英汉老师谈及此事，他说他的朋友——同济大学出版社编辑陈立群先生——也许可以帮忙。经陈英汉老师的介绍，我很快与陈先生取得联系并与之进行了愉快交谈。由于陈先生的支持，《永恒的美丽——美国平民诗选》得以顺利面世。在书稿审校过程中，同济大学出版社的张德胜先生字斟句酌，一丝不苟，对每一篇译文都做了斧正润色，表现出了高度的职业精神和专业水平。

选择翻译诗歌而非小说或其他文学体裁作品主要基于两个原因。一是我从小喜爱诗歌，业余时间也时常写诗。另外，因为诗歌在思想内容、表达方法和语言形式上的特殊性，翻译诗歌比翻译其他文学作品更具挑战性。虽然不少人认为诗歌是翻译的禁区，但中国的唐诗宋词早已被翻译成各种外文而走向世界。同时国外众多著名诗人的作品，包括美国诗人沃尔特·惠特曼、罗伯特·弗罗斯特和艾米莉·狄金森的作品，都先后被译成中文出版，并且广受读者喜爱。诗歌翻译是一个再创作过程，只有通晓两种语言文化的诗人方可为之。在翻译这些美国诗歌作品时，我抱着学习的态度，力求遵循严复先生的“信达雅”三原则,将原作的思想和音韵传达给读者。

出于版权方面的考量，收录于《永恒的美丽》中的所有诗歌原作都源于公共领域。为了便于读者阅读鉴赏和开阔视野，我所选择的诗歌均为短小精悍之作，并且主要出自美国平民百姓，特别是妇女、黑人、印第安人或其他少数族裔作者。书中收集的大部分作品涉及传统普世题材，包括对爱情的讴歌，对大自然的赞美，以及咏物言志和即事感怀。这些诗歌题材多样，流派纷呈，从不同侧面反映了美国平民的生存状态和心路历程，为了解美国诗歌艺术的演变和多元文化发展 提供了一个独特窗口。特别值得一提的是，书中多位作者是 20 世纪二三十年代美国哈莱姆黑人文艺复兴运动时期的活跃分子和骨干成员。其作品对过去一个世纪美国的音乐、舞蹈、艺术、文学、时装和民权发展进步具有深远影响，为黑人文化成为美国当代诗歌和流行艺术的中坚力量铺平了道路。

衷心感谢这些诗歌所有作者。他们的作品犹如散落在文学艺术园地的璞玉，朴实无华，典雅动人，帮助我度过了新冠肺炎大流行期间充满忧虑不安的日日夜夜。我真诚感谢我的家人和亲友，他们的关爱和鼓励给予我温暖和勇气，永远是我前行的动力。在此，我特别感谢我的中学数学老师付文珑先生。他对科学和艺术的挚爱和追求对我的成长影响深远。三年多前通过微信与我取得联系后，先生同我保持着密切交流，对我的译作给予高度关注和积极评价。不幸的是他在两年前突然病逝，来不及道别就离开了热爱敬仰他的家人和分布于世界各地的学生及挚友。

最后，我要感谢玛可辛·G·西尔维曼女士和贝克定及林素芬伉俪。西尔维曼女士是一名多才多艺的独立诗人，三部诗集的作者。虽与我素昧谋面，但毫不犹豫为《永恒的美丽——美国平民诗选》写了热情洋溢的序言。我与贝克定夫妇是相识多年的朋友。贝克定博士的父母是我在约翰·霍普金斯大学求学时的导师。贝克定－林素芬伉俪分别在台湾东华大学和慈济大学教授西方古典文学和中国思想史。他们在序言中对这部选集中收录的美国平民作品给予了高度赞扬，并给予我本人极大鞭策和鼓励。

《毛诗序》阐明了诗歌在社会、家庭和个人生活中的特殊地位与功能：“正得失，动天地，感鬼神，莫近于诗。”而且诗歌可以“经夫妇，成孝敬，厚人伦，美教化，移风俗”。先贤对诗歌的精辟论述同样适用于这部来自美国民间的诗集。在当前这个充满机遇与挑战，希望与困惑的时代，人们向往诗与远方的生活。希望《永恒的美丽——美国平民诗选》能为您“打开一扇心扉”，提供“一方宁谧的风景”，帮助您在喧嚣的尘世中静坐沉思，陪伴您安然度过往后的人生旅程。

李国华

2023 年 1 月 8 日于纽约